NOTHING CAN
BE AS CRAFTY...

An alumnus of IIT Kanpur and IIM Ahmedabad, it was while working with a leading commercial bank that **Ajay Mohan Jain** was inspired to take up writing. He is the author of the bestselling *Nothing Can Be as Crazy...* published by Rupa Publications which is now being considered for a screen adaptation. He lives with his wife Sindhu, and divides his time between Mumbai and Kanpur. This is his second novel.

He can be reached at info@ajaymohanjain.com and www.ajaymohanjain.com.

NOTHING CAN BE AS CRAFTY...

AJAY MOHAN JAIN

RUPA

Published by
Rupa Publications India Pvt. Ltd 2016
7/16, Ansari Road, Daryaganj
New Delhi 110002
Sales Centres:

Allahabad Bengaluru Chennai
Hyderabad Jaipur Kathmandu
Kolkata Mumbai

ISBN: 978-81-291-3760-9

First impression 2016

10 9 8 7 6 5 4 3 2 1

The moral right of the author has been asserted.

Dedicated to
the fond memories of my father, Shri C.L. Jain
on his birth centenary year
(10 February 1914 – 16 January 1998)

Contents

Prologue

Can craze for a pornographic website lead to uncover a high-level scam for siphoning off huge funds?

'I think, basically, we have been able to crack the mystery due to our earlier server room misadventure and experience when we tried to watch such a site from outside the server room by fiddling with the monitoring terminal. This experience only led us to sniffing and ultimately unfolding the scam. See, how ironic it is that craze for the site led us to uncover a high-level scam for defrauding, and consequently saving us from many untold problems. In a way, it became a boon in disguise.'

1

Cal Again

River Hooghly meandering through its course at the far end of the city was looking majestic from the window of my 19th floor office on J.L.N. Road at Maidan. I could clearly see it turning towards the city before Dakshineswar temple and then heading southwards to Howrah through Belur Math. The massive structure of the Howrah Bridge hanging on cantilever and supported only on two sides simply looked marvellous. It was a spectacular sight, to view smoke-emitting steamers lined up at the far end of the Hooghly. On the other end of Hooghly, stood a testimony to modern engineering marvel–a recently constructed all-wired bridge, Robindro Setu. The lush green vastness of Maidan in front of the office looked amazing and a tram rambling through its tree-groves at snail's pace was making it to be a scene straight from fairyland. Left of the Maidan, stood the white-marble building of Victoria Memorial in its all grandeur, with an equally magnificent twirling bronze sculpture of an 'angel' installed at the top of the building. It was the same Cal (now Kolkata) from where I had started my career from an in-house training of FBI (First Bank of India) as Probationer some nineteen years ago in the early eighties. I was so mesmerised by the richness and the warmth of the place that I immediately fell in love with it. I had returned to the place now after nineteen long years, but the city still held the same special place in my heart. The area from Dharamatalla to Park Street still had the same charm for me.

Slowly, the sun was setting down on the horizon and people had started pouring into the Victoria Memorial lawns. Reddish sunrays washing the memorial made it look far more majestic and imposing, making me nostalgic and reminding me of our training days. It seemed as if it was the matter of other day... We had just landed at the Staff College of the FBI to join as POs from all parts of the country; from all shades of lives and characters—men and women, MBAs, CAs, engineers, PhDs, Ranji Trophy and State Hockey players. All were very vibrant, bubbling with lots of energy and expectations—*Grown-ups and yet not so grown-ups*!

During the two years of probation period, apart from various institutional trainings at the bank's training centres, one had to undergo on-the-job training at different branches to get acquainted 'hands-on' with the multifarious activities of the bank. Of the twelve administrative circles of the FBI, in India, I was allotted and assigned North-Central Circle of Lucknow as my parent circle on joining the bank. These circles were controlled by their respective CHOs. Each circle was further divided into operational units of zones for direct control of branches, under their geographical jurisdictions.

Belonging to the second generation city-migrants and a slightly conservative middle-class family, I remembered how difficult it was for me to initially adjust to the free and *bindaas* new environment during my probation days. We had the first taste of it immediately after landing at the hostel for orientation training of our probationers batch. On reaching our hostel, we were served morning-tea, as it was already half past seven. Our inaugural session was scheduled for 9.30 a.m. The atmosphere in the hostel was quite free. People attending other programmes and already staying there, were drinking tea and chatting freely in the corridors. In the opposite wing balcony, a woman in tight jeans, was sitting over the railings casually, with her back towards us, least bothered about her rear view. As the woman was sitting slightly hunched, her kurti was

lifted well above her jeans, revealing the cleavage that led to her bums. Few men in the corridor were just covering their bodies with gowns, without anything beneath them.

Yet, on another occasion, it was beyond my wildest imagination when one day, a female probationer attended the class in totally scandalous, revealing clothes. She was wearing a tightly wrapped, transparent, white chiffon sari, over an equally see-through, white polyester blouse, enhancing her body contours.

Our probation period of two years was full of new experiences and exciting adventures, sometimes embarrassing, along with newfound monetary independence and freedom. Since it gave us the first taste of personal liberty, it was a no-holds-barred time for us. We would not leave anything untried, even keeping our lives and careers at stake. In a way, we were quite reckless. I remember our first puffs of hashish at Victoria Memorial lawns. It hit one of the batchmates so hard that he almost collapsed, gasping for breath. And then the escapades of two other batchmates with a slut behind bushes and later in the night its verbatim narration during the bull session in the training centre hostel room, resulting in total pandemonium at midnight. We were too engrossed in the ordeal to realize that it was well past midnight and that all the commotion was streaming out through the open windows to the surrounding residential area. And when the residents living in the neighbouring apartments of the training centre complained to the chief instructor about the nuisance created by us at the dead of night, we were sternly taken to task and were served the show cause memos for our misconduct, almost putting our careers at stake. I remembered that, in fact, these two were not the only (mis-) adventures while exploring Cal during our training period. Earlier, we had just survived the wrath of a pimp when we unwittingly bumped into one, responding to his luring calls out of curiosity and fun.

We did not realize when two years of our probation period flew past, shuttling from one branch to another for on-the-job training interspersed with institutional training. Time moved on, turning us into matured men, from the free birds of the training period. Of course, some of the batchmates left the bank for better pastures and more desired destinations.

Gradually, we got into the humdrum of routine life and kept moving to different assignments at different places, yet we remained in touch with each other and relived our probation days whenever we got the chance. Our responsibilities at work and in the family were increasing. Yet, we never missed a chance to relax and have fun. We continued our journey at the FBI, hopping from one posting to another; sometimes getting assignments of our liking, sometimes not so desirable, yet manageable.

I had reported at Cal after being relieved from my parent circle at Lucknow. Until then, I had spent most of my time in the Lucknow Circle in various capacities, at various places except my three years stint at a newly started Computers Institute of FBI at Bangalore and special training in computers at IIM Ahmedabad. I was doing well in the circle, when a sudden turn of events, due to politics, led to the ire of the management, and I was continuously under fire from senior management. Added to all this, a slackening in my functioning around the same time, due to an unexpected development in my family, provided my baiters with further ammunition. And finally, the lid was blown off when I refused to overlook and violate eligibility norms and rules for financing a home loan to the relative of a senior.

'Rajesh, did one Mr Verma come to you for a housing loan and you refused to oblige him?' my immediate boss, the ZM, grilled me over the phone.

'Yes sir, he did come for a housing loan, but his plot was an agricultural one outside the municipal limit, and hence was not eligible for a housing loan. So he could not be financed.'

'So what? You know who Mr Verma is. He is very closely related to our senior. I just received a call from the boss that it is to be done. Moreover, your branch is quite short of home loan targets.'

'But how can an agricultural plot, outside the municipal limit, be financed for a housing loan?'

'Who doesn't know all this? See, he has been recommended by the boss...then why are you worried? He would take care of any fallout.'

'Sorry sir, I can't finance housing loan for an agricultural land. I can't do this so blatantly, come what may.'

'It's up to you. I was just advising you as your well-wisher. Anyway, you decide, but then be prepared for the consequences as the boss would definitely get it done.'

'Either toe the line and flourish, or apply reason and perish.' Soon I was given a marching order out of the circle. Thanks to my 'connections' at the central office and my specialized training in computers, I managed to land at Cal, and that too for an important assignment of head of the Computers Group at the Foreign Transactions Monitoring Office (FTMO) of the FBI.

By the time I was relieved and reported at Cal, only few months were left to complete my twenty years of service for becoming eligible for pension. I found the job in the Computers Group at the FTMO quite gratifying and also of my liking. The environment was very professional as the team mostly consisted of highly qualified specialist officials. Besides, I was away from the dirty politics of the circle. Earlier, I was seriously planning to quit the job after completing twenty years of my service, mandatory for getting pension, but with the changed stimulating office scenario and easing of tension at home-front, I was now in no hurry to submit my papers. More so, as my son was yet to complete his engineering degree. Moreover, my friends at Lucknow sounded me against submitting my papers now, as my baiters there were trying very hard to embroil me in some case or the other to fix me up. They were searching for evidence at various places of my earlier postings to find out something, some procedural lapses at least, against me at the behest of the same senior circle functionary. He was to retire in few months' time. They advised me to wait at least until he retired.

2

Different Dimension

The Foreign Transactions Monitoring Office, a central office establishment, was a computerized state-of-the-art office. It was an online gateway and the nodal office of FBI to monitor its foreign currency transactions and deals all over the world. The Director (Foreign Operations), a very senior official of the rank next to ED, headed it. It had a mix of different cadre officers drawn from various circles all over India and had more than fifteen departments spread over nineteen floors of the building. Of these, more than ten departments, like the Cover Department (to make provision and cover foreign currency transactions for any fluctuations in value), Operations Department (for accounting operations), Reconciliation Department (for reconciling the entries), Contract Section (to take care of forward contracts) were directly involved with the foreign transactions operations. As some currency market or other remained open at any point of time, we had to remain open twenty-four hours. Since foreign currency market was very volatile and a single deal could make or mar the business, it was of utmost importance to keep computer systems up, twenty-four hours, three hundred and sixty-five days uninterruptedly, so that the time lag in information transmission was minimum. At the same time, it was also equally important to maintain the secrecy of the foreign currency deals and protect the computer systems from unauthorized access.

My Computers Group at the FTMO was responsible for running of the computer systems at the FTMO. It was entrusted with all the upkeep and the maintenance of these systems and the associated networks (computers networks) on regular basis. Besides, it was responsible for procurement and installation of new systems, as and when required, either for new projects or otherwise for upgradation. It assumed special significance as every employee of the FTMO had at least one internet-enabled networked computer system. Some also had standalone systems apart from networked terminals, depending on the job requirement. Though internet was then just making inroads, but the FTMO network had unlimited internet access.

The scene at Computers Group located on the nineteenth floor was like a science fiction fantasy. Various sections of the group were separated by aluminium-glass partitions and fitted with password-operated doors, concealed close circuit cameras, and movement recording systems. Since it was the hub for all the computer networks—internal as well as external, having satellite connectivity through VSAT, it was full of various computer equipments including servers (main computers in the network) and routers (equipment through which different networks are connected for data transfer), and anybody would be mesmerized by their continuous beeps and flashing LED lights. The main server room was in the most secured area, very isolated from other departments, and generally inaccessible to anyone. Even the system administration jobs were done through remote login by the System Administrator, having limited access rights to main servers. We had a team of our own employees to supervise the maintenance of the systems, but actual maintenance was done by outside vendors, on contract basis. The vendor engineers were deployed on full time basis and reported directly at the FTMO to me. They would go to their companies occasionally for personal matters only. They had their independent regular desks at the department, equipped with networked computer terminals, and all other required devices and gadgets. These vendor engineers were such an integral part of Computers Group that even long after joining the group, I was not very clear who was on our roll. Once, when one of them told me as mere courtesy that he would not be coming in the ensuing week, I immediately retorted, 'But I have not sanctioned your leave, how can you go without proper leave?' 'No sir, in my absence my company will send some other engineer,' and only then I realized my mistake.

The operations at the FTMO—from reporting of any forex transaction taking place in any of the branches to carrying out of various processes (like providing cover for any fluctuation in the currency value, accounting, and then validation of the entry)—were fully computerized. Earlier, it was all manual and reporting was done through mail, telephone and then later through telex and fax. Therefore, it took a lot of time. Later, with the computerization at branch level, it became partially mechanized. Now with the networking of computerized branches and offices, and migration to core banking platform, it has become almost seamless and in real time. Now the forex transactions taking place at branches were immediately converted into data strings (of 'zeros' and 'ones') by the branch computer. The data strings were passed on to respective Circle VSAT located at various CHOs over wired lines (PSTN [Public Switched Telephone Network]). From these CHO VSATs spread all over India, they were transmitted to a nodal VSAT hub at Hyderabad through satellite channel, from where these were sent as signals over satellite channel to Cal FTMO VSAT receiver terminal. These data strings were then extracted and decoded in actual transaction entries at servers of the Computers Group at the FTMO, and then these entries were passed on to different sections for various operations such as providing cover, accounting, reconciliation etc. These entries were then again converted into data strings, and validated at the Computers Group servers and then sent over to the gateway server, for further transmission to the New York Office as data string.

3

Happy Days Are Here Again

'Meet my friend Aishorjo,' my wife introduced me to her new friend.

'Hello, I'm Rajesh. Nice name you have!' I was a bit of surprised by her name.

'Hello! In fact, my name is Aishwarya, but we Bongs pronounce it as Aishorjo, not correct to say we cannot,' she clarified reading an expression of disbelief on my face.

'Great! But how can we do it, pronounce like Bongs?'

'Simple! Pop a rossogolla into your mouth and then try pronouncing my name, and it will sound like Aishorjo only,' and we had a hearty laugh.

My wife was visiting me to do a one-month's refresher course for the University teachers, at Calcutta University. She was teaching at one of the post-graduate colleges, a Christian minority college, affiliated to Kanpur University and decided to continue her job there when I was transferred to Cal. It was her second stint at a permanent teaching job and this time she did not want to leave the job. In fact, this time she took up the job only on the condition that she would not give it up. So, she did not come with me to Cal and I was staying alone as a forced bachelor. Earlier, she had taught for five years before leaving it in 1986 to become a full-time mother. As she had to do a refresher course, she jumped at the opportunity when Calcutta University announced to conduct a one. It was killing two birds with one stone—completing mandatory requirement of doing a refresher course and staying with me. Moreover, Calcutta University was reputed to conduct such courses better than many other universities.

The course proved to be our second courtship-cum-honeymoon as we were free of all strings and worries of life. Our son was in a hostel, doing his engineering course. We were staying in an all-furnished flat from the bank, at Golf Green residential complex, continuing with my South Indian 'dabba' arrangement for breakfast and dinner. And if we wanted anything more, a fully equipped kitchen was there. Moreover, the residential complex had a guesthouse as well, so you could avail mess facility at any time. Our official timings were also the same—10.30 in the morning to 5.30 in the evening—and I made it a point to leave my office by 5.30 while she was here. Otherwise, there was no specific time for me to leave the office in the evening. More so, because there was nothing better to do at home when you live on your own. Since my office was at Maidan and her Academic Staff College was at Rajabazar Science College Campus of Calcutta University, we were on the same metro route. We would leave together in the morning; me getting down at Maidan metro station and she at the next station—M G Road station. In the evening also, we would try to catch the same metro on our return. It was such fun and excitement to board the same metro from Maidan station, in which she would already be. It was all pre-fixed and synchronized—the time, the coach she would board. I would wait for her metro at a pre-determined point—near the staircase on Maidan metro platform, and board it when she waved from within like a youngster on her date with her boyfriend. One day, unaware, we were seen waving to each other by one of my office colleagues. The next day office was abuzz with the grapevine that I had a female-friend, as they all knew that I was staying alone. It reminded me of our courtship days at Lucknow, when we would meet daily after our working hours at a pre-decided place. I was posted there after my confirmation in the bank and she was doing her research at the Lucknow University. I would wait for her at the famous 'Lovers-lane' of Hazratganj that gifted the unparalleled pleasure of 'ganjing', a cool stroll without any specific purpose. Sometimes, we would meet at Mayfair theatre. There also, one day we were caught waving like this from across the road by my boss and the next day he indirectly pulled me to be clear and precise about the place and time to meet people. As she was there for a short period at Cal, and had come on scene suddenly, the thrill and spark was no less than that of our courtship at Lucknow.

Our romance started the day she arrived at Cal. After dropping her home from the station, I left for office. On my way back home in the evening, I realized that I had left soft porn Russian channel REN TV on. This sent a shiver through my body. I thought this would unnecessarily spoil her mood when she watched TV and I would be on her firing range and face a volley of piercing questions from day one. Apprehensive of her rage, I very nervously pressed the bell of the house and anxiously waited for her response. But she gave a tight hug and a volley of hot kisses...(Perhaps, that is why it is said that nobody can ever predict a woman's behaviour and response).

Later, of course, one day she mentioned that now she realized why I did not call her so often in Kanpur.

On some days, we would not go back directly home, and instead, roam around the place from Maidan lawns to Park Street, to Esplanade, to Camac Road and so on just like teenagers, hand-in-hand, completely oblivious of the world around. We could do all these antics as we were new to the place and not many people knew us, so there were no middle-class hang-ups (of what people would say). Nothing much had changed at the place since I had visited the place for the first time for my in-house FBI training some nineteen years back except some malls coming up and the metro becoming functional. In fact, all the big Malls and brand-showrooms were located in the close vicinity of my office at Chowringhee. Other things were more or less the same—from hand-drawn rickshaws or to the all white chana-jor-garam-wale. The area from Dharamatalla to Park Street still held the same charm, as it did nineteen years back. The sights of hand-drawn rickshaws returning on the side lanes of Chowringhee and the sounds of the brass rickshaw-bell were too fascinating to be ignored. The mammoth Raj-time buildings with broad windowsills had a very distinct flavour and elite feel to the place. The windowsills lining the ground floor of the buildings were used by pavement vendors to display a variety of wares—from old books to fake foreign items to herbs to shoelaces. Equally eye-catching were the assorted leather-items and readymade garments shops on the other side of the pavement.

While roaming in the vicinity of Park Street area, we would as usual come across some well-built, large-checked-tehmad-wale fellows (trademark of the pimps) but nobody cared to whisper their usual phrase of '*Laggega*', which I had often heard from them during my training days. May be because I was with my wife. Since she had often heard stories about encounters with these pimps from me, one day my wife insisted that I should show her the place where we lost our money, our dignity but thank God, not our virginity to these tehmad-wale while strolling with one of my batchmates on the sidewalk of Park Street near the Middleton Row crossing during our training time. (Grown-up yet not so grown-up, to be discreet always). It so happened that out of curiosity my friend on the spur of moment just responded with '*Kahan hain?*' to the luring call of '*Laggega*' of one approaching tehmad-wale, and when on parading the girls before us he realized that we were not actually interested in their '*ek-dam first class ka maal*', I swear, we had it. Immediately, seven to eight goons surrounded and bulldozed us. Losing whatever money we had, perhaps, we escaped unharmed and unhurt due to their business 'ethics'. I could still feel the chill in my spine when we reached the place. It had changed totally—flooded with neon lights and all crowded, as 'Sourav's—The Food Pavilion' had come up there. There was no sign at all of a dimly lit and all deserted side lane where we were almost butchered nineteen years ago. In fact, it was exactly where the eatery had come up now. As I was showing the place and narrating the incident by indicating and mocking through my hand to my wife, suddenly one cop appeared on the spot asking for our identities, suspecting our relationship. When I protested how he dared to point a finger on a married couple, he changed his stance, 'So what? You were making indecent gestures at the public place.' In fact, he was sure that he could extract some money by threatening us to book us for making vulgar actions at a public place, but luckily we had our I-cards with us. I was amazed at the alertness and swift action of our law-enforcing agencies that they could pretty well suspect a decent looking married couple but nobody had come, when pimps were actually parading the girls and manhandling us openly.

Visiting one of the most recent malls one evening she was surprised when I suggested going down to the ground floor by the escalator. 'But how you will go? It's very steep also from the fifth floor to the ground floor.'

'So what? It's meant for going down only. Come!' She was dazed at my initiative remembering how scared and reluctant I had been to go down by the escalator few years back at Hotel Taj, New Delhi for some function. Then I was helped by a lobby attendant to reach the basement by the escalator, almost being dragged, clasped under her arm, my eyes closed.

'When did you become so bold? What is the secret?' she pulled my leg.

'In fact, while visiting malls, I saw lots of kids bungee jumping without being scared, and that inspired me. So when a new mall came up adjacent to our office, my daily routine for some days during lunch break was to go there, and just practise few rounds of going up and down by the escalator every day, just to get over my fright.'

'All crap. You need not tell me all that bullshit, I can understand very well what inspired you to make the trips on the escalator, so that while going down on the escalator you could enjoy the saucy top view of the females moving up on the adjacent one.'

4

At Razor's Edge

I was slowly getting accustomed to the totally computerized environment of the FTMO. Though I already had a fair exposure to computers from my IIT days and later had also undergone thorough training while at the FBI Institute of Computers, and at the IIM, Ahmedabad, but the scenario had changed completely from then. Gradually, I was getting used to this.

My immediate priority, apart from routine monitoring and initiating the process for procurement of new servers as replacement for old servers, was to resolve the critical issues of network speed (computers network speed), which was getting far slower during day time.

'Sir, we are frantically trying to ascertain the reason for the network to slow down (data transmission to slow down) during day time. We have observed that it gets slower particularly during the time slot of 11-11.30 to 3.30-4 in the afternoon,' reported the senior engineer of the AMC vendor.

Responding to the observation of senior vendor engineer that it was getting slower particularly during the time in the afternoon, I expressed my amazement, 'But is it not very surprising that network gets clogged during day time whereas most of the major world currencies transact during our night time?'

'Yes sir, very true. We have also checked that external data strings density is much more during the night than that in the day. So, if at all any jamming is to take place, it should take place at night. That means it is not due to the external network, but the internal network of our office,' vendor engineer further concluded.

'But to improve the functioning of our internal network, we have already replaced the Ethernet coaxial cables with the latest faster optic-fibre cables,' I interrupted.

'Sir, it has improved substantially since then, but we have added many more users to the network after that to take advantage of increased capacity of optic-fibre technology. So, the load on the network has gone up many times, but still it is far-far better than those Ethernet days when it used to clog almost totally during the day', joined my junior Rajendran. 'But that is not the issue. The issue is why is it getting slower during the day, during the lean period than in the peak hours of night,' Rajendran elaborated. Rajendran was a telecommunication engineer in the Computers Group. He was a young, smart Malayalee, born and brought up in Delhi. Since he had joined the FBI directly from the college very recently, he was a 'baby', not only of the group, but of the whole FTMO. He used to do all the running around, and was almost indispensable to the users because he was available on the spot. Therefore, he had unhindered access to anyone.

'Yes, in fact it's a real riddle. But how do we solve it?' I said, a little desperately.

'Don't worry, sir! We are trying to figure out the reason and soon we will be able to pinpoint and solve it,' Rajendran said hopefully.

During the next weekly review meeting with the DFO, when the issue was raised, I assured him, 'We are working on it sir, and hopefully, soon we will be able to fix it.'

'But to improve the functioning of the network, we have already replaced the old servers (main computers in the network) with the latest state-of-the-art technology servers that have external memory array boxes (boxes having huge external memories modules to enhance the memory of main computer), and Ethernet with the optic-fibre cables,' the DFO raised his genuine query.

Getting wiser from the knowledge passed on by Rajendran, I immediately used it to impress the boss, 'Sir true; and these steps, no doubt, have definitely improved the capacity and the speed of the network many times, but the issue is not that. The issue is why is it slowing down during the lean period, that is during the day, in comparison to the peak hours at night.'

'Yes, exactly! You are very right, but is it not strange, these things are happening?' Our boss apparently was satisfied with my intricate knowledge of the issue and command over the situation.

'Sir! But God willing, soon we will be able to solve this riddle.' I again assured him without really having any clue about it, behaving in a typical bureaucratic style of 'never-say-don't know' or 'unaware'.

In the evening, after returning from the meeting, I apprised the group members about the discussions I had had with the DFO. 'Sir, don't worry. We are very close to figuring out the reason; rather, we have almost figured it out and solved it. Let us see how the network behaves tomorrow,' Rajendran said very confidently. In fact, in the afternoon, I had seen them working on the servers before going to the meeting.

'Why? Have you done something?' I was inquisitive.

'Let us first see the effect tomorrow then I will let you know,' he insisted.

'But I hope system is functioning properly, that is my only worry right now,' I expressed my concern.

'Oh, it is functioning as usual. No complaints so far from any quarter. But as it is already past seven, the crucial period of 11 a.m. to 4 p.m. for checking slower speed is over, so we will have to wait till tomorrow morning to check the speed,' he said and added further in a fading tone, 'But my worry is about the boss,' swallowing last few words.

'What is that about boss?'

'No-no, nothing...We will see tomorrow.'

'Okay. Let us wait till tomorrow.'

Next morning when I reached my office, I saw through the glass partition of the department from the corridor, a lot of people thronging my desk and having heated arguments with Rajendran and other group members. I felt a chill thinking that the network had collapsed. Reaching my desk, I anxiously inquired, 'What happened? Is the network functioning all right?'

'Network is functioning alright, rather it has become very fast. However, we are not able to access all the sites which we were accessing until yesterday. Someone is being mischievous with the network,' one of them commented. I was relieved that the network was not only functioning all right but it had also become faster.

'But all the required sites are available and accessible, and, that too, faster. Tell me, which other sites are required for the job and not available,' intervened Rajendran very spiritedly.

'We require a lot of sites to access, from time to time, depending on the demand of the job,' somebody replied very diplomatically.

'But tell us at least few sites, which you require right now, apart from the sites available,' I tried to reason.

'But how can we tell you now in advance what sites we will require during the course of the job,' replied someone.

'Then let us know the additional sites, as and when required, and we will do the needful,' I countered.

'But then, we will miss the bus by the time we get access, you know how fast you have to react in the forex deals,' he tried to emphasize the crucial nature of the operations.

'Okay, I agree. But tell us some of the sites, which you generally access during the course of the job or at least those sites, which you have accessed in the past. Give me the names of these sites in writing. Only then, we will be able to do something,' I contended little firmly.

'No. No need to oblige us. We will go to the DFO and report the matter,' and left threatening us.

As soon as they left, Rajendran told me why they were so agitated—they were unable to access the share market sites, which were blocked now. They were all indulging in online trading in the share market, simultaneously, while doing their online jobs. In fact, barring very few people, it was very lucrative business for most of the people at the FTMO. That was why the network was turning slower, particularly between 10-10.30 a.m. to 3.30-4 p.m. Apart from these, some popular and known porno sites were also blocked, which was another reason why some of them were unhappy. 'Oh, no wonder that was why one of them once asked me if I was interested in buying and selling shares,' I recollected. (Of course, I had a better pastime of completing my book).

'Yes, they also asked me vaguely once if I had the FBI shares, and what other shares...' Rajendran recounted his conversation.

After knowing this, I felt relaxed, as they would definitely not go to the DFO for this, at least not immediately. But no sooner, Rajendran started explaining his modus operandi to detect and fix it, that I got a call from the PA to the DFO, telling me that the boss wanted to see me.

On reaching there, I felt relieved when I saw only Mr Sikdar leaving the DFO office. No one else from the staff was there. 'Oh, the network has really become faster, but I am unable to access some sites. But never mind, they are not that important,' the DFO said looking a little perturbed and uncomfortable.

'No problem sir, I will send Rajendran. Please tell him the sites you...'

'No-no, don't send him. You know what he did last time.' He snapped at me. In fact, some time ago, the DFO had happened to stray into some porno site and that had become his default site. He had tried to fix it himself but when he could not, he had called Rajendran on the pretext of making one other particular site as his default site. But Rajendran had not been able to help either. In fact, nobody could do it, and ultimately the computer had to be replaced. In the process, it became somewhat public, which was very embarrassing for him. After that, he started blaming Rajendran squarely for all the goof-ups.

'Okay, tell me the sites, and I will check them personally,' I suggested.

'No-no, leave it…I was just wondering if I needed to check something on the internet any time soon,' he was visibly in a fix.

Noticing his dilemma, I immediately came out with a solution, 'Yes sir, you must have unhindered, unlimited access to the internet. I suggest you should install an exclusive terminal with complete, separate internet connection. Perhaps, that will do.'

'Oh yes, that will do. In fact, that is more rational,' he said with a great sigh of relief.

When after going back to the department, I narrated the whole conversation to Rajendran, he gave me a knowing smile. 'Why do you smile so mysteriously? Anyway, tell me how did you get the inkling to this?' I asked Rajendran his secret.

'Yes, whenever I visited these people I noticed that they would immediately close certain windows on their computers and that made me suspicious. In fact, once when I asked about this, I was told that forex deals were not supposed to be divulged. But as I had unhindered access to their desks, in the process, sometimes I could notice the content of the window before it would be closed. First, I did not take serious note of it, but then I thought, if so many people were using this site or such other sites simultaneously, then how heavy would the network be loaded, and then we decided to try filters on such sites and see the effect on the speed, and it worked.'

'Oh, so you took advantage of free access to anybody. Good, as we have been able to solve this issue how about now taking up the matter of upgrading terminals (improving capacity by improving processor or enhancing memory or both) of some officials who keep pestering for it? Mr Mullick, for one, reminds me every now and then to upgrade his PC, whereas even the AMC vendor engineer reported that it does not require upgradation as its configuration (capacity specifications) is more than sufficient to handle the job.'

'Sir, this time when he calls you for this, just tell him that his printer will also be have to be replaced, along with his PC,' suggested Rajendran. He paused and added, 'Or why should we even wait for his call, you may call him now, say this, and see how he responds.'

As soon as I told Mr Mullick this, he immediately changed his stance, 'Mr Rajesh, I think now it is more or less working all right, with the network speed improving. So now you need not change anything.'

I asked Rajendran what magic it was. He coolly unveiled yet another secret, 'Sir, all these people are having the same or similar printer model at home, requiring the same type of consumables—ink cartridges, paper, etc., so they cannot afford to get their office printer replaced for obvious reasons. They would never agree to this. Moreover, now with so many of the sites which are often used by them simultaneously being blocked, a higher configuration PC, anyway, is not needed.'

'Great, as until now they would open and work simultaneously on so many windows, then they would keep complaining that memory was insufficient; processor was slow and so on. So, with these sites being blocked now, the daily noises of insufficient configuration and upgrading of PCs from others would also automatically subside. What a respite!' I said joyously.

'Hopefully so. Let us see for how many days, as these people are not going to take it lying, especially people like Mr Sikdar, who has a huge exposure in the stock market. But yes, some respite, at least for now. Moreover sir, you have very tactfully handled and solved the problem of at least the most important affected party, the boss. So you can take it easy,' and after a pause added in a receding low tone, 'But be prepared to face the music later.' Mr Sikdar was a senior officer and quite an influential person from an old landlord family in Burdwan, having roots locally. He was highly qualified, having a masters degree in Physics from Berkeley, US, and later a PG Diploma in Computers. Highly qualified and a computer buff from core, he had been deeply involved with the computerization of the FTMO operations from the very beginning; from selection and purchasing stage to implementation and customization of the system. He seemed to be quite close to the DFO. He was said to not only have the largest portfolio of shares, but also managed others portfolios. Being from an affluent family he was living a cosy life, with interests in vintage cars and antiques.

Without heeding what Rajendran said, I shot my next worry, 'Now, tell me one more thing from your omniscience...,' again falling back on Rajendran's insider info system.

'What is that sir?'

'See, we have received a note from admin, saying that over the past few months, our photocopier expenses have just doubled! In fact, as a special case, we have been provided with a heavy-duty photocopier as we need to photocopy urgent matters at odd hours. So, we should have been judicious in its use, but it seems to me that it is being misused.'

'Sir, it would have been okay if the special printer's usage was restricted to photocopying the staff members kids' school and college projects. But, there is more to it. I have seen photocopy vendors outside getting documents of other sections photocopied here through our men and charging for them.'

'Really, that is too much. They are photocopying our office documents, using our printer and our material, and charging us!'

'Shocking as it may seem, it is a fact sir!'

5

Honeymoon Continues

Much of the grounds surrounding Victoria Memorial had been now covered and enclosed by a boundary wall. The new Elliot Park, developed close-by in Maidan across Tata Centre, had become a centre of attraction for youngsters. With thick trees and bushes all over, and a boating facility inside, it was heaven for them and hence one of the most sought after place. As my wife was in a holiday mood, despite her being in the refresher course, one evening we too decided to visit the place. It was well maintained and manned. Eatables were not allowed inside the park, but people were freely taking 'muri', buying from chana-jor-garam-wallas standing outside. With the sun setting down on the horizon, the day was getting softer and many people had started pouring in. Mild, pleasant breeze was blowing, and the reddish sunrays reflecting from the white marbles of the nearby Victoria Memorial, were making the atmosphere romantic. In the front of the park, people were sitting in groups, including families with kids playing around. Some people were busy jogging while others were doing yoga and exercises. It was a different scene at the back of the park. It was filled with young people barring few like us, who had happened to stray to this side of the park. Even guards manning the park were not seen around this side of the park. Though it was getting dark we could still see couples lying on the grass, kissing or petting. Occasionally, the sounds of heavy kissing punctuated with moaning were quite audible from behind the bushes. Though my wife did not want to stay there, but we saw a vacant bench, and decided to sit there for some time. Thanks to our surroundings, soon, we too were lost in ourselves, enjoying a little naughtiness. When we heard some female haggling with a person behind the bench, perhaps a whore trying to extract extra money from the client, we thought it was time to leave. When we reached at the turn of the walkway to the front side of the park, suddenly a guard appeared from nowhere on the scene, asking '*Bakshish, saab*.''Why? What for?'

'*Saab*, you enjoyed the place and I was guarding...'

'But we were just sitting there.' '*Saab*, don't say that at least. I was guarding you all along so that you would not be disturbed.' He very tacitly made it clear that we were being watched all along while indulging in our own naughtiness. I gave him a fiver when my wife, embarrassed, elbowed me to stop arguing. But he refused to move and said, '*Bass saab, itna hi kya?* There are other guards also.' I had to add another fiver to get rid of him. While moving towards the front of the park, we met one of my wife's local course-mates. She was with her family and her eyes widened in disbelief on seeing us emerging from the back of the park.

'Coming for the first time?' 'Yes, we have come for the first time and thought it would be nice to take a complete round of the park,' my wife very smartly clarified taking cue from what she was hinting at. Taking leave of her, we came out and decided to have snacks at Ganguram's before boarding the metro from Maidan station. Moving towards Ganguram's,

I saw Rajendran coming from Tata Centre with his girlfriend, who worked at the Tata Centre, and going towards the park. I thought he did not see us. But it was not so, when the next day he mischievously commented that he was under the impression that only youngsters visited that park.

On way back by metro, my wife asked, 'Where is the Millennium Park?'

'It is just by the side of Strand Road facing Hooghly. But who told you about it?'

'My friends at the course mentioned it. They were also saying that you could go across the river Hooghly to Howrah station from there by ferry.'

'Oh yes, you can take a ferry from Babughat there. Once, when during Durga Puja holidays I was going to Kanpur, there was so much traffic on Howrah Bridge up to Strand Road, that I had to take a ferry, leaving the cab there, to cross Hooghly to catch the train.'

'Can we go there day after tomorrow for a ferry-ride across the river Hooghly, as it is an off for me for project work?'

'But I don't have much leave left now.'

'Can't you take "French" as you used to, while at Lucknow?'

'Those were different times when we would go to the boss on some pretext or other and get the applications approved personally in the course of discussion, and then after leaving his chamber, we would never give it to the one responsible for keeping record of leaves. As a result, employees would think that an officer had gone on some official job, whereas the boss would think that the concerned one was on leave, and would never ask for him. If ever reminded of the absence, we would submit the application saying we forgot to deposit it, otherwise tear it off after some time. That is not possible now.'

'Then what? How can we do it?'

'Let me see tomorrow how it can be managed.'

Next day at the office, I called up one of our computer system's vendors from whom we were buying the systems, 'I would like to visit your factory for a pre-delivery inspection tomorrow.'

'Oh, you are most welcome sir! What time would you like to come?'

'I would like to reach your place by 11.30 in the morning. Where exactly it is located?'

'Oh, don't worry about that. We would send our car to pick you up from your office.'

'Okay, but then I would like to be at your place sharp 11.30 and finish the job in the first half of the day itself, as I have some other urgent work to do.'

'Absolutely, no problem sir! It would be arranged just like that only.'

Next day, as fixed, I visited their works and finished the job by 1'o clock. When he insisted I have lunch there, I told him, 'My wife must be waiting for lunch, actually. She is here nowadays. Only thing, I would like to be dropped at home.'

'Oh, wonderful! It is nice that the Madam is also here these days. Sir, on Saturday evening, we are launching our new software product at Hotel ITC Sonar. It will be our pleasure to have both of you there for cocktails, followed by dinner. We will feel obliged if you could keep that evening free for us. Of course, I will be coming to your office tomorrow to invite formally.'

After going home and having lunch there, we were dropped

by the same car at Babughat by 3'o clock. On the way, I suddenly remembered, 'But when will you do your project work for which you have been given off today?'

'Oh, I have already completed that. In fact, my project is related to banking. As all the reference materials related to the project are readily available in various pamphlets at home, it did not take me much time and effort to complete the project. Now, you will have to get it typed in your office tomorrow. I will need five printouts. Hope you will get them spiral bound too. After all, impression counts too,' she added.

'Great! You are a genius. You completed the whole project without visiting even a single place or meeting a single person! I wish your students will also learn from you how to do things so effectively and smartly.'

'Not only that, I have collected enough material to do a minor UGC research project. I will get a handsome grant for doing this project, and will get a chance to visit Cal again,' she boasted.

'Superb! No wonder, that is why we have had so much research post-independence, but...no Nobel Prize,' I taunted feeling a bit jealous as she had turned out to be smarter than me.

'Perhaps, but we don't do that much lobbying at international levels,' she said matter-of-factly, in a mature and thoughtful tone, like other intellectual Indians.

It was a bright sunny afternoon, when we reached Babughat. She insisted on having *daab* first. While she was busy getting it, I phoned my assistant at the office to get certain things done. Drinking *daab,* we took a stroll around the place. Nothing much had changed in the last nineteen years since my visit to the place during my training period, except for a new park and the area around jetty being now cleared and properly constructed. She was thrilled when the buzzer rang and the anchor of the ferry was lifted, and soon the 'ghar-ghar' sound of the steamer engine was lost in the loud 'hoohoo...' sound of the high tides of the river Hooghly. River Hooghly was sparkling in the orange-yellow light of the setting sun. Sunrays reflecting from the long trail of waves and bubbles left behind by the ferries appeared to be dancing on the waves. Looking from the ferry one could not resist admiring the engineering marvel of the massive structure of the Howrah Bridge. It was a scene to be relived. By the time, we reached Howrah station across the river Hooghly, it was getting dark and we decided to have tea in the new IRCTC Food Plaza on the extended Howrah station. While sipping tea, I suddenly remembered, and called up my office to enquire whether the instructed job had been done, 'Hullo,... *(blah, blah, blah)....'*

'But sir.... *(blah, blah, blah)....'*

'You could not complete even that also. This is not good. Where is...'

'...*(blah, blah, blah)...'*

'What, he has already left? It is just 5.40! Was he waiting for clock to strike 5.30? ...And oh yes, I will be delayed here as I am continuing with the job. So today, now I won't be coming to the office and going directly from here..', and I switched off the phone.

'Very smart!' my wife remarked admiringly *(or I thought so)*.

'Oh, yeah...but slightly less than you.'

'How?' she asked me very intently, thinking she was really one-up.

'I attended office—may be for some time; I also visited the vendor's factory, but you have completed your whole project, sitting at home.'

'But you are no less. Nobody can beat you in managing office through phone; you are a master in it, a real tele-manager. Remember, how effectively you used to manage the Petrochemical Complex branch near Gorakhpur from home by phone, when on some days you did not feel like going to the office. In fact, you started your own tele-banking (managing) much ahead of the actual advent of the tele-banking facility in the banks...' and we shamelessly laughed at our self-proclaimed smartness.

'While getting down at the ferry terminal, I saw some ferries going on the other side also.'

'Oh yes. They go towards north Calcutta, beyond Howrah Bridge.'

'Oh, then it must be quite exciting to see and cross under the Howrah bridge. We must go. Moreover, we would get a feel of old north Calcutta.'

We went again to the jetty and took a ferry to Bagh Bazar, the farthest terminal on the other side of the Howrah Bridge. The ferry for crossing the Howrah Bridge was smaller and was deep sunk like a submarine, with only the top portion of the navigation cabin being exposed above water. It was designed to have a very small part projected above the water so as to cross under the Howrah Bridge without any problem. Unlike the previous first ferry, it had no overboard deck to sit on. One had to sit inside it below the water level and could even splash the river water from the ventilator standing on the seat. We were spellbound when we passed under the gigantic Howrah

Bridge. We could even feel its vibrations from down below.

After getting down at Bagh Bazar terminal, we took a cycle rickshaw to Sovabazar metro station. On the way, we had glimpses of north Calcutta lanes which evoked memories of Raja Rammohun Roy, Vidysagar, Tagore and the likes. While passing through the place, I just remembered that Sonagachi, the well-known red-light area of Calcutta, was also on that side. I wished I could have seen the place at least, but I could not risk doing so with my wife. Moreover, I was told that the sightseers visiting the place for the sheer feel of it were totally unwelcome and hated, and outsider women were absolutely 'no-no' there. It was all business and they had their own norms, howsoever strange, applicable there. Now reminded of the place, how could I miss my friends' stories during our training?

◆

As soon as we reached Sonagachi by a taxi, we were surrounded by a host of pimps...one of the them came forward to take us and show us the maal (girls) up the street. One we selected, he quoted high rate beyond our budget. He clarified that rates included cleaning, and cap (condom) as well. We told him that we had already brought our condoms. Then he suggested, 'You go for little older ones and the rate would fall within your budget.' But when we did not agree to his advice and showed reluctance, he came with a unique win-win solution—one girl per two persons, of course one by one. The deal was settled for about 70 per cent of the original rate per person. What a trade!

...While waiting for his turn in the hall, one fellow asked the pimp, 'Why do the girls here have only first names, and no surnames?' 'Because it does not matter as long as you have a

"saleable slit", it is one and the same; it is the only religion here.'

....When during the session, one of them demanded to a girl's breast, she refused very shyly, 'How can a girl become so familiar in the first meeting itself...' It was the joke of my life. Later we came to know that this was not included in the package and rates were for only the main act.

...When one other fellow complained that it was all too mechanical and all over in no time—just lifted the dress and lay spreading her legs... He was clarified that the deal was not time-wise but just per prick. However, he was offered to have another go if he wanted, and he replied he would rather prefer doing himself.

I wonder whether these women take up the trade just to fill their bellies or have insatiable lust for more money. But one thing I am certain of is that we should feel obliged to them. Because of them only, dignity and integrity of lot many other women remain intact and safe. No doubt, they are unknowingly serving the society, and that too totally unsung.

◆

After reaching Sovabazar metro station, we took a metro to Tollyganj to reach Golf Green.

'What should I wear for cocktails on coming Saturday? I do not have a proper dress for the occasion?' she grumbled as usual.

'I do not understand how you ladies never have clothes but are still always found to be well dressed. Wear anything. You have so many! Moreover, it is just a company's product launch party and not a marriage reception, so how does it matter what you wear,' I said ruefully.

'Let us go to Camac-Elgin Road this evening. I saw some very big showrooms there.'

'But you will find only imported and up-market items there.'

'There is no harm in visiting them. At times you get very good things well within your budget. At least you will get to know the latest "in" things and what is happening around.'

In the evening, we started looking at the shops from one end and reached a well-known showroom. While she was busy in finalizing some lingerie and dresses, I went to the other side of the shop, where apart from lingerie, there were sex toys too. When I asked the salesman about these, he looked at me blankly, perhaps deliberately, and very innocently said, 'What is that? You talk to my boss,' and he called an executive. When I repeated my query about the sex toys, especially about inflatable dolls, he gave me a look from head to toe and very diplomatically said, 'Sir, about these you will have to speak to my director. At the moment, he is not here, you leave your number; he will give you a tinker. In the meanwhile, I will show you our great collection of some unusual undergarments and accessories, no less than those.' He took me behind the partition and started showing me some arbitrary items like cane sticks, leather chains, some gloves, boots, bands, anklets and so on; perhaps sadomasochism accessories, apart from jazzy undies. When I enquired the price of one zebra designed underwear, having hardly any cloth and more of multi-coloured rings, it was exorbitant—about five hundred.

'Why are they are so expensive? They are not even branded. What is so special?' I was inquisitive. 'Sir, only when you take off your pants you will realize their speciality,' replied the executive coolly and I did not know what to say. I bought a slightly cheaper underwear and rushed out of the shop to avoid further embarrassment of being noticed there by some acquaintance. My wife's bill naturally ran into thousands, and I already had my five star cocktails beforehand any ways. When she saw my expression being distorted, she coolly said, 'Don't worry, this month I shall pay your credit card dues, from my TA-DA of the course. Moreover, most of these items are lingerie...for you only.'

On our way to catch the metro, I saw similar underwear being sold on the Chowringhee pavement at less than one tenth of the price I had paid. (And the so 'special' underwear was never worn again as my wife found it quite disgusting).

The cocktail party at the five-star hotel was also an experience in itself. Instead of a software product launch, it looked more like a fashion show. Most of the women, irrespective of their age, were scantily clad, flaunting body-hugging outfits. Others were also trying to compete and look equally jazzy in their best of dresses. The chief hostess was looking stunning in a revealing low-cut black cocktail dress, which buttoned up at the back. Apparently, she wore nothing under her shimmering, all-too-transparent evening dress. There was a PowerPoint presentation on the software, after which a small questionnaire was given to the audience on that software. And lo, I did not know how, my wife won for giving correct answers and was given a decent prize. During cocktails, my wife elbowed me, pointing towards one woman bartender who was wearing revealing clothes and was hopping and mixing too much with the guests while serving margaritas and martinis in Ibiza style. My wife gave me a hard stare and moved away visibly raged when she came to me and started chatting. I gestured my wife to keep cool. I murmured, 'Must be a "prof" but don't make your disgust so obvious,' when she left. All the guests were given parting gifts. It was very nice of the company's director to see us off at the porch, 'Should we collect the purchase order tomorrow, sir...?'

Life is a big unsolved puzzle and you never know what is there in store for you. Sometimes, certain events in life may not look favourably, but may ultimately turn out to be boons in disguise. For example, they wanted to throw me out of Lucknow circle to north-east as vengeance, but then I landed at my dream destination of Cal, all away from the dirty politics of the circle, and was enjoying our second honeymoon. I wonder whether it is the circumstances that lead you or it is your dormant desire for something, which leads you to such circumstances, enabling you to fulfil your dreams. I imagine that many a time circumstances take the shape that you desire them to be, consciously or unconsciously.

Man is never satisfied with what he has, but he wants the best of both the worlds. He always wants to eat the cake and have it too. So was I. It was so far so good, but there was one thing that was continuously bugging me—my project of writing a book (my first one, in which I had made a lot of progress on the plot, till I joined back on my last posting, after a long leave. I was working on the plot, thereafter). But the project had taken a back seat as a result of all these activities and was badly suffering. Reaching home late after all the *fatrugiri* in the evening, even if I would try to sit alone for some time on my laptop, I could not; as she would immediately start grumbling that I did not want her to be there. If I insisted on going ahead with the book, then she would try her best to distract my concentration—rest her head on my shoulder, narrate her day at the institute, try to show some interesting thing in a magazine, or even put off the lights. She was in a total holiday and romantic mood, and after her working hours, wanted me to be with her all the time. Still, I would somehow snatch a few moments and try to key in few lines every day. In the process, at times, I would doze off half lying while struggling to write. Writing is a very obscure process. Sometimes, you may write pages at a stretch but on some other occasion, you may feel totally handicapped to even scribble a few lines. On one such day, I dozed off in a semi lying position thinking about the storyline. Slowly, my senses were blurred and soon I slipped into a deep slumber. I felt as if I was being softly clasped. Lo and behold! I started feeling light and elated with a lovely feeling of gliding over the clouds, some sensation, some fondling of.... Whether it was in dream or actually happening, I could not make out but that heavenly feeling of enjoyment was definitely there. Slowly, I realized that now my index finger was rubbing against something soft and sticky. What...and then suddenly I did not know what happened, I felt a sort of flash in my head, and at once, I was out of trance, fully awake. I pushed her aside, getting out of her embrace, and jumped out of the bed as I had a plot for my book. You never know when you may get a wonderful idea, often you get it at odd places, odd times...may be at the peak of such an intimate encounter, and then you would want to jot it down before it slips out of your mind. It is ironic, but that was what had exactly happened to me, and I did not want to risk losing my idea even at the cost of disruption during those intimate moments, as making love was in your hand but you may not get that idea ever again. In the morning she tersely complained, 'Do I not understand that you no more want me here,' when I got irritated about her occupying the bathroom for too long. I knew it was her late reaction to last night's incident. *(It often happens with me that I get a flash of ideas during or just after a sexual encounter as if it opens up my third eye.)*

Time passed very fast. We did not realize when the thirty days of our second honeymoon, in the guise of a Refresher Course flew over, and it was time for her to return to her teaching assignment at Kanpur, and me to carry on as a forced bachelor again. I wondered whether it had been a refreshing course for her or both of us.

6

Tender Committee Not So Tender

The process for procuring our new, main server as a replacement for the old ones had already been initiated by constitution of Selection and Tendering Committee,[1] as approved by the central office for the purpose. I was Member Technical & Secretary of the committee. In the routine weekly review meeting, the DFO informed us that central office IT Dept people wanted to discuss certain things about the proposed tender for our new server and for that, they had arranged a video conference just after the meeting.

'Yes sir, they have some reservations about specs (specifications–technical specifications or configuration) firmed up by us. They are of the opinion that these are too stringent and ambitious. They want to dilute these,' I apprised him as I was handling the committee formed for the purpose. Apart from the DFO and me who were from Cal, all other

---

[1]For the procurement of any system, a Selection and Tendering Committee is constituted by the appropriate authority comprising of Chairman, Members, and a Member Technical & Secretary as per the CVC guidelines. The Member Technical & Secretary drops the specifications in consultation with the other members of the committee and the details of the tender are finalized by the committee. Then the tender is floated.

members were top bosses from the central office, Mumbai. As per the CVC guidelines (Central Vigilance Commission guidelines), for the expensive, high-end system (of more than a crore), only top bosses of the DFO rank, except member-technical, could qualify to be members of the Selection and Tendering Committee.

'What do you feel?' asked the DFO.

'I think we cannot dilute these keeping in view the future requirements and scalability of the system.'

'Let us put across our contentions in the video conference.'

When we reached video conference hall, the DFO felt very happy to find the new longer cable of the webcam-mike-pod which was earlier a little short and the DFO sitting at the other end of the table had to lean over to come into webcam view. I grinned when someone remarked (in appreciation?) that it was done by me.

'Oh, don't you know, Rajesh is from IIT!' commented the DFO enthusiastically, as if for extending the webcam cable one had to be a B. Tech from IIT!

The matter was discussed threadbare in the conference with IT Dept people in Mumbai. While they did agree to have certain degree of scalability in the system, they tried to stick to their guns for diluting the specs in the name of optimum configuration. In the course of discussions, it was ultimately revealed that they had discussed the specs with certain reputed vendor, who opined that it was very difficult to meet those specs. 'But how can we decide our requirements based on the opinion of some single vendor. We cannot dilute our specs if some particular vendor, howsoever reputed and big he may be, is not in a position to meet these. Let us see who comes for the technical bid. If no vendor qualifies in the technical bid, we will refloat the tender modifying our specs,' I contested. Though it was not at all ethical or done thing to discuss the tender proposal with some vendor, but being a small factor, I had no guts to question this, and thought better to keep quiet on this issue.

After some time, we received a message from the central office stating that it was not possible for the top bosses, members of the selection and tendering committee, to be all present for the tender committee discussion and meeting in Cal. Moreover, it was getting difficult for the IT Dept in Mumbai to coordinate and expedite the tendering process as the Member Technical & Secretary was posted in Cal. Therefore, it was decided to reconstitute the committee, replacing me as Member Technical & Secretary and co-opting another official from the IT Dept in Mumbai itself in the position. 'The new Member Technical & Secretary would freeze the specs for the tender.' Read the communication.

7

A Win-Win Situation

Totally fused and hurt by the treatment meted out to me in the matter, I took leave and soon left for Kanpur. Relaxing over breakfast, my wife broached the matter of availing our overdue LFC facility.

'Our LFC is overdue and just because of your dilly-dally I am not going to forego it this time. We must avail it without any if and buts,' forewarned my wife. Earlier, on many occasions we did not avail our LFC or HTC (Home Travel Concession) facility.

'Yes, definitely. But we must plan and chalk out our programme well in advance.'

'How about visiting Singapore, Thailand, Bangkok, etc.?' suggested my wife immediately.

'But you can go anywhere in India only, and will get reimbursement up to the farthest point here,' I clarified.

'Then how are other people going to these places outside India but close enough?'

'People are even going to USA why only nearby places.'

'Really! Has someone gone?'

'Yes, recently Mr Sikdar, of our office returned from the States, on availing LFC.'

'Then how is everyone going to the places outside India?'

'There is a catch in the rules and they take advantage of that clause. As per this clause, one can take a circuitous route by a lower mode of conveyance and class than entitled, and claim re-imbursement of the fare for the farthest point touched by the entitled mode and class, if it is less than the actual expenses incurred in the circuitous route. So, travel agents arrange tickets by such lower modes for the farthest point in India, and as a part of circuitous route they arrange travel for such tourist destinations abroad,' I explained the modus operandi.

'Then what is the problem?"

'Who would go to some obscure place as the farthest destination; and that too by lower mode and class? Are we taking LFC for rest and recuperation, as defined in the scheme, or for some exercise?' I reasoned.

'But what do others do?'

'They simply don't go to the farthest destination.'

'That means they don't touch the farthest destination.'

'Exactly, hence reservations for this scheme. Some smarter people even cancel the ticket and get refunds.'

'Oh my Gosh! That is a fraud straight away,' my wife said visibly shocked.

'Yes, very much, but very few have guts to do that. Of course, very few touch such obscure farthest destinations physically.'

'Then how do they show their presence at the farthest point...?' asked my wife naively.

'Normally, it is not required. In any case, as a matter of abundant precautions, the travel agents manage and provide some local sightseeing ticket or some other receipt as proofs of going there. '

'Well, we cannot do these things. Let us actually keep it to India, and visit some of our relatives, especially some of our family's children,' suggested my wife.

'Yes, our nephew Sunny was insisting that we should go to his place, when he visited us the last time. He has again reminded me over the phone, when he called me to tell that he might be going to Singapore to scout for some data duplicating software.'

'Okay, we will visit Sunny as part of our LFC. One destination—Ahmedabad, at least is final. Now we will not be foregoing our LFC this time,' she said very relieved.

'Right, what other places?'

'Let us then visit western India, covering various places like Ahmedabad, Baroda, Nasik, Mount Abu, Udaipur, etc.,' proposed my wife.

'Okay, done. But LFC will take care of our travelling fares only. What about other expenditure? How do we take care of these expenses?' In fact, this had been one of the main reasons, though unsaid, to skip LFC at times in the past.

There was total silence for some time before my wife came up with a suggestion, 'Let us utilize part of my salary up-gradation arrears for the purpose.'

'Wonderful, what an idea!' I exclaimed greatly relieved.

'But I am yet to receive these actually,' she clarified.

'Why, what happened? Have you not enquired in your college office?' I asked.

'These at the office told me that they are yet to get it from the government,' she said.

'Then let us enquire from the concerned government department,' I suggested.

'In fact, they were telling me that unless you personally go there and grease their palms, it won't be passed,' she said ruefully and further added that even her colleague Professor Sharma had not got it.

'Then ask Prof Sharma. Both of us can go.'

Next day, Prof Sharma and I went to the concerned government department and enquired about it from the official dealing with it. At first, he did not bother even to look at us and continued to work with his head down in a file. When Prof Sharma repeated his query, he replied very tersely that he had lot of other work to do before he could take up this job. This irked Prof Sharma to no end, 'Oh, you people don't do anything without tipping. Is it fair?'

'You people also run coaching classes instead of teaching in the college. Is that fair? Anyway, leave these things; there is no point in useless discussions. See, both of you are entitled to approximately rupees eighty thousand as arrears, and even if it gets delayed by one more month, you will be losing eight hundred rupees as interest at one per cent rate per month. If you want, your work can be done immediately in four hundred rupees. This way both of us stand to gain. Just think about it. A perfect win-win situation'. The professor had no answer to it.

8

Those Were the Days

'You know Rajesh, I have now drawn pension for more years than I drew salary from IBI (Imperial Bank of India),' Mr Banerjee, our neighbour at Kanpur, reminisced when I visited him. Mr Banerjee had worked for many years in the IBI and perhaps, he had retired before the IBI was nationalized in 1955.

I had gone to Mr Banerjee's house to collect some items, which he wanted to send to his relative in Cal. Earlier, when I had been transferred to Cal and he had come to know about it, he had immediately given me reference to one of his relatives working in FBI, in Cal. It so turned out that this man was also posted at the FTMO. When he came to know about it, Mr Banerjee requested my wife to ask me to carry some gift items for his relative whenever I happened to visit Kanpur. Incidentally, Mr Banerjee was the one who played an important role motivating me to join the FBI. He told me about the glorious past of the FBI, when I received their offer. Though I would not say that he was instrumental in this, but this was also one of the considerations, apart from the main reason of my weak health at that point of time. My doctors and family had advised me to switch from all strenuous engineering industry jobs to a desk job in banking to improve my health. Thus after working in two engineering companies, I landed at FBI and it was my third job. And they proved to be quite right when I gained good 15 kilos of weight, (from 49 kilos to 64 kilos), within six months of my joining the bank.

'How sir?' I asked Mr Banerjee.

'See, I am ninety now and I retired at the age of fifty-eight. So I have already drawn pension for thirty-two years whereas I drew salary for about twenty-five years.'

'Why, did you join late?'

'No, I did not join late. But during the IBI days, initially people used to join on contract basis and then after ten to fifteen years of service they would be confirmed in the regular service. You know that they emphasized so much on good handwriting that on joining the IBI, for the first six months, one had to only practise handwriting. It was must as they were required to maintain handwritten accounts ledgers and these money transactions had to be clearly mentioned, without over-writing.'

'Oh-ho…no wonder that is why I came across some very beautifully written old ledgers of the early twentieth century while I was involved in the bank's history project. Now, one cannot even imagine these things. We have transformed from class banking to mass banking and personalized banking to mechanized banking.'

'Yes Rajesh, we used to know each and every customer personally. Now the customer may not enter the branch at all and transact all his business without visiting branch through franchisee kiosk, internet and ATM.'

'Not only that, soon with the rapid progress of technology, you may not even require to key-in your password at an ATM, as it will automatically verify your face biometrically as soon as you stand before it. This will also eliminate altogether any possibility of fraudulent withdrawal by stealing the password.'

'Yes, otherwise also, things are totally different now. See, you get a fix annual increment as a matter of right, but in the IBI days, it used to be a big ritual and nobody knew whether he would get any annual increment; and if at all, then how much. On 31st December, it used to be a big show. In the banking hall, a huge multi-tiered dias would be erected. An agent would sit on top of it, on the tier below, the sub-agent would sit, and so on. Everybody would wait for agent *'angrez saab'* to arrive and to preside and declare increments. And at last, around mid-night, a message would be received that *saab* was too occupied in the club and not coming from there and in his place the sub-agent would announce the annual increments. The Steno of the *saab* from the bottom of dais would call names from the roll one by one, and the *saab* would declare the increment of the employee. And can you imagine that most of the time he would say 'nil'. And even those who were lucky enough to get, would get increments in paise—one paise, two paise, three paise...The highest increment would be in some annas,' Mr Banerjee said spiritedly remembering his good old days.

'What a pity, Uncle! To hear that "nil" you had to wait till past mid-night.'

'Anyway, that was our usual time to reach home. But we had a lot of respect in your locality people would point and say "see, her husband works in the Imperial Bank."'

'Why "her husband" and why not the man himself?'

'Because they would never see the man himself. There was a joke that on one holiday when kids saw their father at home they asked who that man was, as they had never seen him earlier. He would leave home before they woke up and come back only after they were fast asleep.'

'I have heard that the *angrez* agent was also never seen, even by the staff. Of course, in my first branch building at Deoria (a district headquarter town in eastern Uttar Pradesh), I saw that the anteroom to the Branch Manager's chamber had a staircase, opening directly from his upstairs residence. So if he wanted, he could have avoided being noticed by anyone, in his coming and going. Though I had gone there in early eighties for my first branch training but the branch building was of British time,' I added remembering my first branch training.

'Not only that, even at some branches like Kanpur Main Branch, the agent's residence was across the road and people used to say that there was an underground tunnel beneath the road connecting the branch to the agent's residence as nobody would ever see *angrez saab*. But one thing these *angrez saabs* were very particular about, was that the cash-book should be tallied and signed on the same day, whatever time and wherever they were, even at a club.'

'Yes, Bade-Babu of my first branch, who was of Imperial Bank times, told me about the same practice. He also said that even people dared not pass through the road in front of the branch,' I remembered this from my first branch training days. No doubt, memories of the first branch, or a first job, like that of first love, can never be erased from one's mind.

'As a part of the protocol, even the district administration official on joining their position would call on the Agent,' Mr Banerjee recalled the practice prevalent from British times until early fifties.

'Yes, my father's friend told me that after confirmation when he joined as Police Kaptan (Superintendent of Police) of Gorakhpur, the IBI agent was next to the Commissioner and Collector whom he called upon.'

'And having an account with Imperial Bank was a privilege.'

'Yes sir, my father used to say with a great pride that he had a current account from the Imperial Bank days,' I endorsed him.

'Currency printing and management was also with the Imperial Bank before formation of the Reserve Bank in 1935.'

'Yes, and perhaps, the designation of Treasurer, used till late seventies, came from there,' I added.

'Yes, it has a long history and has evolved over a period of about 200 years from British Raj bank to people's bank, and has a very strong foundation,' said Mr Banerjee with great pride.

'That is why sir, it has such strong systems and procedures in place, and is also greatly acknowledged by the DBOD (Department of Banking Operations) of the RBI,' I again endorsed him.

This gossip would have continued, but I had to stop and take leave of him, as I had to catch the train for Cal that evening, to reach office next morning on Monday. Nevertheless, I had all the admiration for Mr Banerjee to have such loyalty and dedication to the institution he had served with unflinching faith and trust. Perhaps, that generation was different and that was why it commanded such respect as an institution.

9

Adda Incorporated

'Hi, Rajesh! Where were you? In Kanpur?' my Lucknow Circle fellow, Bajpai who was my junior by a batch, and a head of another department, (Reconciliation Dept), at FTMO, greeted me in the office corridor after lunch. I felt somewhat relieved on seeing him as I was very uncomfortable and out of place ever since after returning from Kanpur, in the morning.

'Oh yes, I just returned this morning. How are you? What news?'

'Nothing as such, as usual, People were trying to sympathise with you at the Officers' Lunch Club the other day, shedding crocodile tears. Bastards!'

'Must be enjoying the incident.'

'Leave those bastards...one bugger even whispered—what does he think of himself? Anyway, forget them; let's go to my desk and have a cup of tea.'

'Okay.'

On reaching his desk, he ordered tea from the canteen over the intercom and resumed our conversation. 'So you enjoyed your trip to Kanpur?'

'Well, in any case, I had to go to Kanpur as it was overdue. So I thought—let me take a break now.'

'After how long did you go to Kanpur?'

'After a long time—more than a month and half.'

'Great. Very long time by your standards, is that right? How could you hold it for such a long?'

Bajpai, who was very lively, outspoken and always full of filthy language, emitting abuses, was very free with me. We could talk about anything, anytime. In fact, more often than not, we talked nonsense, just to relieve our tension. They knew that I used to visit Kanpur almost every month unless my wife happened to visit Cal. Cal-Kanpur was less than a twelve hours overnight journey by Rajdhani Express.

'Yes, to be frank, it was very difficult. Even after fifteen-twenty days I start feeling moist seeing anything worth...'

'So how many times did you actually enjoy?'

'To be precise, five times,' I replied after taking some time, mocking as if I was counting on my fingers.

'How?'

'See, very simple—during the three nights and four days stay—thrice at night, one quickie on reaching early morning by Rajdhani Express and one shot in the afternoon on the last day.'

'Good going.'

'But the limit is when even at this age you have wet dream, and that too at odd places like in the train after enjoying sex five times.'

'I think you very well qualify to endorse and promote Viagra,' he laughed. I was relieved of all my tensions after this bullshit. In the meantime, tea had also arrived and another officer, Das from my batch from the Orissa circle, who normally every day used to have tea with Bajpai after lunch, joined us. He was another Bajpai type officer, and had a very good relationship with him. From his face itself, even at this age, he looked out and out crazy. Mischief was written all over his face. He, like me was a 'forced bachelor', as his family was in Bhubaneswar.

'What Das, looking very tired?' Bajpai teased Das.

'Oh yes. As you know these days, my wife is here. *Woh sali chhodti hi nahi mujhe.* She doesn't leave me for a moment as she doesn't have anything else to do except...I wonder what she does there in Bhubaneswar...how she stays there for so long without me,' Das said mischievously.

'Oh I see, you have all our sympathies, poor chap...cha... cha...cha,' commented Bajpai mockingly.

'Today, I bluffed her while leaving home for office saying I would be late as I had very urgent work in the office. Now I am planning to go to Rajesh's house, so that I can take a break.'

Our conversation came to a 'sudden-death' with a phone call for me from the DFO secretariat.

10

Higher the Position, More the Ego

'Next Monday, they are holding the tender committee meeting to discuss the tender proposal at central office at 3.30 p.m. We had some discussions during our last video conference with them about the specs proposed by us for the tender as they had some reservations on these,' the DFO recalled the last discussion we had with the IT Dept, Mumbai, telling me about the meeting.

'Yes sir, they were of the view that the specs proposed by us were too stringent and ambitious. They wanted to dilute these, but we contended that we cannot, keeping the future requirements and scalability of the system in mind.'

'Oh definitely, we must keep our plans for expansion in mind and hence must have cushion and scalability in the system.'

'Though they did agree to have a certain degree of scalability in the system, they tried to stick to their guns for diluting the specs in the name of having optimum configuration.'

'What is the period for which you want to have scalability?' asked the DFO.

'Sir, say for two to three years, as we have economic life for three years in which the cost is depreciated. We should not look beyond this period as the set of variables change and technology gets obsolete. We should start our search for new system after two years and it should be in place within a year thereafter, so that we should be able to recover full value of money. At the same time, we should ensure that our system does not get out-dated, and we should not lag technologically. Sir, this is the optimum time horizon. I feel, based on this, we should decide about our configuration.'

'Very true. They also mentioned something about discussing this with an MNC vendor.'

'Yes, they had also discussed the specs with a reputed MNC vendor, who according to them, opined that it was very difficult to meet those specs.'

'How could they discuss tender proposal with a vendor in advance? It was totally unethical,' retorted the DFO.

'Moreover, how can we decide our requirements based on the opinion of a single vendor, howsoever reputed and big it might be? We cannot dilute our specs if some particular vendor is not in a position to meet these,' I added.

'Yes, how anybody else can decide about our requirements? Even the central office IT people can't. After all, we are the end users, and we know the best. We will decide specs for our system, nobody else will,' exploded the DFO. 'You also come along with me for the meeting on next Monday.'

'But sir, I am not a member on the committee now,' I expressed my constraint.

'So what? It is my prerogative whom I take with me to assist me,' the DFO retorted again. Perhaps, he was more hurt than me by my removal from the committee and wanted to take me just to keep his ego up. He was a very senior official originally from Calcutta Circle, having all his roots in Calcutta, and the senior most among all his peers. He was in his final lap of his career, doing the last assignment prior to his retirement.

'In fact, I'm told by someone that they are very soon going to send a team to Singapore, the hub of investment banking, to study systems with various investment bankers there, and also visit works of some of the MNC vendors located there. This will also be decided in this meeting. Everyone has his own interest and wants to include his candidate in the team, but I would make sure that you are included in the team going to Singapore."

'But sir, I don't have a passport.'

'Whatttt...?' the DFO almost jumped out of his chair in disbelief.

11

How Defunct Committee Can Meet

'After returning to Cal your one point agenda should be to get your passport without delay,' the DFO commanded in no uncertain terms during our flight to Mumbai to attend the tender committee meeting at the central office. He further added that through this time he would see to it that the matter of finalizing the team for Singapore does not come up.

On reaching the central office, there was still time for the meeting, we went to IT Department just to say hello. On seeing me there, Head (IT), (head of the IT Department, central office Mumbai), commented tersely, 'I think we have a new Secretary to the tender committee.'

'He has come to assist me in the deliberations. Moreover, he will be coordinating and supervising the installation of the system in Cal. His involvement is very important,' the DFO replied.

'Oh definitely, we should take advantage of his expertise though he did not think worth joining IT Department and share his expertise with us then,' taunted Head (IT) little sorely, remembering the past when I did not join IT Department. In fact, I was identified and transferred from Lucknow Circle to IT Department central office, Mumbai. But after reporting at Personnel Department, central office, Mumbai, I did not report at IT Department, and instead I managed to change my posting to Computers Group, FTMO, Calcutta. This I did purely for two reasons—one, Cal was directly connected to Kanpur on main Howrah-Delhi route, so it was easier to commute; two, somehow, I felt that Mumbai was not a place for an easy-going person like me. But, these people took it otherwise, and Head (IT) still carried the same hard feelings.

'Before the formal discussions starts, I have one small observation to make,' the DFO said at the very onset of the meeting.

'Yes. What is that?' the Chairman of the committee asked.

'Nothing very important but a little procedural.'

'Is it in order to discuss the specs of the proposed tender with any vendor?' the DFO asked coolly.

'We just asked for some clarification,' the Head (IT) intervened.

'Even small clarifications?' the DFO insisted.

'Many vendors visit our department and in the course of general discussions they might have asked general questions, and not specific to this tender,' the Head (IT) tried to justify actions of his department officials.

'But then can we be guided by the opinion of a single vendor while drawing the specs for the tender? And that too by ignoring our own requirement?' the DFO questioned further.

'It is not the question of ignoring our requirement, but our specs should be just optimum and not very ambitious as there cannot be any limit to it,' insisted the Head (IT).

'But we must keep at least our near future plans for expansion in mind and hence must have cushion and scalability in the system,' the DFO shot back.

'What is your time period for which you want to have scalability?' asked the Head (IT).

'We have an economic life for three years in which the whole cost gets depreciated and at the same time the technology also becomes totally obsolete. It becomes almost impossible to maintain the system after this period. Ideally, we should look for a two to three years' time period so that we recover the full value for money, and at the same time we should not lag technologically,' elaborated the DFO.

'Sorry, to intervene in the discussion gentlemen,' interrupted the Chairman, 'It is perfect to have two to three years' time horizon for scalability. But before that the first issue of discussing the specs with the vendors is a very serious matter.'

'Is it not the blatant violation of CVC guidelines?' the DFO immediately tried to get hold of the chance to settle the scores.

'Yes, I feel, we should not proceed further with this tender committee as it would be a grave violation of CVC norms. I think the whole exercise should start afresh, with a new tender committee,' the Chairman gave his final view.

There was stunned silence, as even the DFO never expected such an extreme decision. 'As nobody has to say anything further on the matter, the tender committee stands dissolved, and the meeting is adjourned,' the Chairman gave the final blow.

On the return flight to Cal, the DFO asked me to get ready with the alternative solution, start working for suitable servers on hire as replacement to the existing ones, as these had already lived their lives, and now he was not sure whether we would get new ones in time. 'Start scouting for suitable rental servers immediately on your return,' emphasized the DFO.

'Sir...'

'By the way what is the position of data backups? How these are taken?' asked the DFO considering the risk involved with the old servers.

'Sir, backups are taken in the morning and then in the evening.'

'But if something happens in between, then what is the recourse?' asked the DFO little worriedly.

'Normally, it is available on the server as it keeps updating the stored data, but if something drastic happens in the server, especially, with its memory, then it becomes difficult to retrieve that data.'

'Oh, then it is quite risky to continue with the old servers. What is the solution? There must be some way out,' the DFO asked anxiously.

'Yes sir. I have heard about some real time data duplicating software. They store data on a separate smaller machine exclusively meant for this on real time basis. In fact, we were thinking about these.'

'Arrange for demo of this software on our return,' commanded the DFO.

12

Grapevine Unlimited

'How was the meeting yesterday?' asked Bajpai when we met in office next day.

'Cool! Again the committee has been dissolved,' and I narrated verbatim the whole proceedings of the meeting to him.

'So the Boss ultimately had his way,' commented Bajpai when I finished my narration.

'Oh yes! What news here?' I asked.

'Grapevine was in full bloom here. It was a burning topic at the FTMO yesterday that why the DFO took you to the meeting when you were not a technical member on the tender committee. Everybody was making wild guesses... bastards. One bugger said that you had worked with him earlier, someone said that both of you were from the same alma mater. One bugger was even of the opinion that you might be related to him.'

'Oh, no!'

'As people were quite worried about your proximity to the boss, one of the bastards told them that he has inside information that people in the Lucknow Circle were working overtime to fix you up and soon you would be nailed down,' Bajpai said in a worried tone.

'Why are you sounding serious?' I probed Bajpai.

'No-no...just like that. I was just wondering did he say so simply out of frustration and jealousy or...?' said Bajpai.

'What frustration?'

'Bugger, as if you don't know. Here everybody is suffering and is frustrated because of you. They curse you, as you have blocked all the sites, "fu**er, I cannot watch those fu**ing *Aartis* (porno site)". People cannot indulge in online share trading either,' Bajpai exploded, and then in a very low tone asked, 'How is the boss managing?'

'Has been given a direct link itself from the....' I said almost whispering.

'Oh got the secret! No wonder you are his pet,' said Bajpai enthusiastically. Then, after a pause, he warned me, 'How about people like Mr Sikdar? I have heard he has the largest portfolio of shares... and he is also managing others portfolios. He is also said to have dealings in foreign stocks. I swear these people are definitely going to screw you one day.'

In the meantime, Das also joined us. Just to tease him, Bajpai said, 'Oh today you are looking very fresh.'

'Oh, that sucker has gone,' Das bantered.

'Who?' I asked as I could not get him.

'Oh, my madam. That is why I am fresh,' Das said naughtily.

'Then you should look dull, missing her,' I said.

'Well, that is the paradox of life. When she was here, I started getting bored and restless after sometime. The same thing again and again. Now when she has gone, I don't know what to do, again left to fend for myself,' Das explained his philosophy in his own way.

'Very true, it's natural,' Bajpai endorsed Das's view of life and then turned towards me, 'Buddy, do something, at least for Das's sake. We are starving for *Aartis* for so long.'

'Yes-yes...please,' Das also echoed Bajpai's demand. I kept quiet.

'Since now it cannot be done as such, it cannot be reversed altogether, what I suggest is that you could remove porno sites filters quietly, say after seven in the evening,' suggested Bajpai when I kept quiet.

'I suggest something still better. You won't have to do anything. You just allow us to sit in the server room for some time in the evening. That's all, rest we will manage,' Das suggested.

'How?' Bajpai asked naively.

'Simple. There must be some terminal in the server room to monitor (incoming data signal) before the application of these filters. This terminal must have unrestricted access to the internet. There we can watch *Aartis*,' Das gave a very smart solution.

'Great! Cool idea. Moreover, the server room being soundproof, hissing-and-kissing in the Aartis will not go out,' Bajpai said excitedly.

'Still better... If that terminal can somehow possibly be linked to some terminal outside,' Das came out with further refinement to his idea.

'Oh, he is very competent technically, he will definitely do something. Let him think and arrange,' Bajpai said inflating my ego and we dispersed, as he had to go for some meeting.

All the while, Das's idea—if that terminal could somehow possibly be linked to some terminal outside—was resonating in my mind, challenging me on my face. 'After all, data duplicating software would do what—nothing but linking and mirroring one terminal to some other terminal,' I thought to myself. 'Would this be an answer to Das's idea,' I wondered.

After coming back from Mumbai, I started working on two things—one, to search for suitable servers on rental basis as replacement for our existing servers; two, to assess the necessity and utility of having real time data duplicating software and the capability of such software with different vendors. For rental servers, I had started preliminary discussions with various vendors and for data duplicating software, I asked a vendor to organize a demo at our office.

13

Another Showdown

After the share trading site row, I was very cautious in dealing with the staff members, as I did not want to have another issue with them. However, I was again forced to take a stand when they approached me for providing few PCs for their union meet, as I had no authority to allow anyone to take office property outside the premises.

'But so many officers have PCs at their homes provided by the office,' they grumbled.

'They must have taken prior approval from competent authority to have there office PCs at homes for official use,' I clarified.

'Yes-yes, we also know how much office work they do at home, when they do not have full time work at the office itself,' and they left in a huff threatening to check who was doing what.

'Sir, perhaps, you did not do the right thing by bluntly refusing the staff's request for loaning three to four PCs for their union meet. In fact, they were asking for the PCs for few days and we could have easily obliged them,' opined Rajendran, when I did not accede to the union's demand.

'As such I was not against it, but as you know, we have only all-new, packed PCs which have been bought and are kept here for the new project being launched this week. Moreover, this should have been looked into by Admin and not by us. How can we allow anybody to take any office property out of the office premises? We have no authority,' I clarified expressing my inability.

'Oh, Admin people played their cards very well and safely, throwing the ball in our court by saying that it was Computers Group's prerogative for anything to do with computers,' Rajendran was little bitter about the Admin's plans.

'In fact, Admin people should have consulted us instead of sending union people directly to us. We could have easily arranged three to four PCs by hiring them. What would be the harm, when anyway have had so many systems on rental for so long?' I lamented.

'Exactly,' Rajendran echoed.

'Later, I sounded them also about it but they did not seem inclined to this,' I added ruefully.

'Oh, they had no stakes, but as far as we are concerned, I feel we have further antagonised the staff. They were already furious after their share trading sites were blocked,' professed Rajendran.

14

Hanging in Balance

Once my LFC was approved, I called my wife and enquired about her salary arrears.

'Why, what happened now to your salary arrears? We personally got it passed from the Govt. Directorate the day I went there with Professor Sharma,' I asked my wife, when she told me she was yet to get her salary arrears.

'In fact, orders for payment reached the college the very next day, but it so happened that from that very day the college office stopped functioning normally, and fate of all such matters is now hanging in balance,' told my wife.

'Why, what happened?'

'As you know, my college being a Christian minority institution, it is controlled and run by a Church in this area. But there is another church, which has been claiming control over it, and the tussle for control of college management by two warring churches was going on for a long time. Suddenly, in the last month, the other faction appointed its separate Principal and locked the office. Since then there has been total deadlock and everything has come to a standstill,' my wife said.

'But what is the root of this dispute?' I was inquisitive.

'As I understood from one of my colleagues, who is close to churches' affairs, the whole tussle is to get hold of innumerable huge properties left by the British Anglican Church. The Church of this area contends that it is the rightful owner of all these properties lying in its area after the Anglican Church left, and became non-existent in India. But, the other group governed by the other Church says that it is not so, and they have some order of the Anglican Church passing the rights of these properties to them. After the British left India in 1947, the warring groups did nothing to claim these properties. However, with huge increase in property prices, both the groups are now claiming these properties as their own,' she said.

'Oh yes, even the FBI has been in possession of some of these properties ever since on rental, but everybody, including myself, thought that these properties belonged to FBI and it was the actual owner. Only recently, the FBI has been asked to vacate these. So that is the reason,' I said. 'What could be the solution?'

'One solution could be, as suggested by my one other colleague, that some autonomous agency under overall control of government like Wakf Board may be formed to takeover, control, and manage all such properties left by the Anglican Church. He contends that after British left India, whole India belongs to all Indians, and that means that everything is to be controlled and managed by the rightfully elected government. So, it does not matter where it lies. On the other hand, how anyone can pass on his rights when he himself was not the rightful owner of the thing? So anyone claiming have acquired the rights from a body, which itself was not the owner, cannot be valid and hence it cannot be accepted. The best thing to do is to create an independent body to control such disputed properties.'

'It seems to be, perhaps, most logical.'

'Any way, how will we manage miscellaneous expenses during our LFC?' asked my wife, sounding a little worried.

'Don't worry, I will take a personal loan,' I replied.

'But you never told me about it earlier,' complained my wife.

'It's not available as a staff loan on a concessionary rate of interest. Everyone has to pay the commercial rate of interest,' I clarified.

My wife further asked me to also keep a slot for finalizing my niece's marriage proposal, during my stay at Kanpur while availing the LFC.

15

Good Old Days

I had gone to Kanpur on my way to avail the LFC as well as to finalize my niece's marriage proposal. There I came to know that Vikas was posted at Kanpur itself. We had done our agriculture-intensive branch training together during our probation period at Miranpur, a small kasba about twenty-five kilometres from Bareilly, and had had a great time together. When I gave him a call, he immediately said, 'Let us meet and have a ball.' Though I was talking to him after quite long, but there was no dearth of warmth and bonhomie, and he was still chirpy and young (at least at heart). He was staying alone in Kanpur and his family was back in Lucknow, continuing the kids' education. When I suggested a dinner together, he immediately came with an offer, which was difficult to refuse even at my age. 'See, I'm staying alone here. So, tonight let us have a stag party at my place and revive memories of our good old days. I will call all other friends who are here.'

'What stuff on menu?' I bantered.

'Anything, you name it. Of course, BF and so on...'

'*Baas*, that's all!'

'No, if lucky, you may have a "live" (peep in) also as bonus.'

'What?...Really!'

'Yes, if you are lucky as I said.'

'Is it like spotting a tiger in a sanctuary?'

'Yes, somewhat like that.'

'But how is that possible?'

'Find for yourself when you come in the evening.'

'Okay, see you in the evening.'

I met Vikas after a long time, but found absolutely no change in him. He was as excited to have a stag party as he used to be, during our probation days stay at Nirala Nagar, Lucknow. There, our house became a major meeting point for the freak-out sessions, where boozing, dancing, BF watching had become a routine. One other fellow from those days, Sanjeev, was also there, apart from few other guys whom I had not met earlier. Things had changed drastically from those days now. In those days, to screen BFs, we had to call a video-operator, who would come to our place with all his paraphernalia—TV and Video-Cassette-Player along with X-rated soft-pornographic videocassettes. After setting up the equipment, the video-operator would go to sleep in our house, leaving us alone to play the BF cassettes. He would carry back all his paraphernalia in the morning. Scenario had changed with the advent of CDs. Now, there were no such hassles; you could play BF CDs on TV, laptop, etc., etc. Now with the arrival of internet, you do not need CDs even, as you can access innumerable pornographic net sites on the internet. Though at that point of time, internet had arrived, it was not easily and readily available. It had not become a part of our household use. So, from 35mm porno films days, it had come to videocassettes, to CDs and now to internet. Even the BFs had changed drastically since then. What was only heard of then, now all was readily available—pornography with Indian backdrop. Now, not only did it come with regional tags like Malayalee, Punjabi, Bhojpuri and so on, but even with city tags. Still, the production quality was not comparable with the foreign ones.

While we were enjoying booze and BFs, Vikas's mobile rang. It was a call from Lucknow head office, regarding housing-loans progress.

'Sir, in fact, I'm having a meeting...with one of the very reputed builders here,' Vikas told the boss at Lucknow in a very low tone, as if he was really in a meeting.

'..........'

'I can't tell you now, but I'm trying my best. I will call you tomorrow morning,' Vikas whispered again.

'.....'

'Good night, sir!' and he disconnected the phone.

We continued our session, but for a while, our discussion turned towards going-ons in the office. 'See, it is 9.30 in the night and the bugger wanted to know the progress of housing-loans. As if, there is nothing else to do. No family, no other responsibilities. Have they gone mad?' I said.

'In fact, all the pressure is on the middle-rung officers. The top bosses just fix the targets and coolly monitor them. The lower level people start acting as middlemen and agents and have best of both the worlds—oblige their bosses by getting new business for meeting their targets, and earning the builders' favours for getting their loans sanctioned. They eat the cream. Its the middle level officers who get all the heat and dust,' Vikas erupted in frustration.

'And you are solely responsible for the loans sanctioned by you, if something goes wrong. You will be held accountable and responsible, if the loan goes bad,' I added.

'See, how Mishra is suffering for no mistake of his. People under him, first misguided him about worthiness and the credibility of the prospective borrowers, got loans sanctioned, and then enjoyed the booty from the borrowers. Now, these very people are giving evidence against him in the vigilance case. What a pity!' Vikas said in disgust.

'I think, if you have no personal interest in loaning, the best thing is to play the ball away from your court like my ZM at Lucknow used to do when I was ES there. He had given standing instructions to me that no loan proposal should fall in his sanctioning powers discretion. His modus operandi was very simple. If it was at the lower end of his sanctioning powers band then the loan requirement was reduced so that it would fall under the discretion of an officer, one level below him, and if it was at the higher end of his sanctioning range, then it was raised, so that it would fall under the discretion of a senior official. If by any chance, any proposed loan fell in the mid-range of his sanctioning powers, and which could not be moved up or down, then the prospective borrower had it, as it would never be sanctioned. That was the best thing to do,' I sprinkled some drops of wisdom from my acquired treasure of experiences of working with others.

'But not everyone could do it, not at the branch level at least, as the buck stops there. Not everyone has guts like you, who did not sanction a top boss's relative's housing loan, and you could get away with it; as you had specialized knowledge of computers to fall back upon. In fact, in a way you were rewarded—you got the plum posting at the FTMO Cal,' remarked Vikas little dejectedly.

'Oh, forget about Rajesh's ZM, he had no match. Bugger was not only a very cautious player but a very smart one too. He would always get things done through the ES and later he would deny that he had ever given any such instructions to the ES,' added Sanjeev.

'In fact, many times as the ES, I had to face wrath of others, as people thought that I was the real culprit behind all that,' I recalled ruefully.

'And do you remember my ZM at Varanasi, another crazy fellow! He wouldn't call anyone during the day, and then he would start calling them after 7.30 in the evening. And by any chance if you had left the office by then, then you would have a taste of choicest blessings (foul language)—*main yahna ma** raha huin aur tum whan abhi se hi biwi ke pallu main ch*** rahe ho*. Nobody would dare leaving office before him,' recollected Sanjeev from his days at Varanasi.

'This organisation is really great where the elder brother can continue to be in service even after the younger brother has retired,' added Vikas in a lighter vein.

'By the way, how are you finding it there at the FTMO, Cal? I have heard that there also you have gone full steam,' asked Vikas gulping his last sip from his glass.

'I am thoroughly enjoying the work and trying to do my bit by improving network functioning, nothing more.'

'Oh yes, I have heard that you have applied filters on internet to restrict access to pornographic sites. People are restless without these, and cursing you left and right. Great! In fact, I was wondering why you would be interested in BFs, when you had an unlimited access to the internet and could access any number of these sites. Now I realize…,' teased Vikas.

'I had no other alternative.'

'Oh, you can't keep low, that is not there in your blood. Here, in Lucknow Circle, these buggers are still trying very hard to catch you for some wrong doings in your earlier postings,' Vikas remarked.

In the meanwhile, our booze stock on the table was getting over and so Vikas got up and gestured me to come with him to the adjoining bedroom to get a fresh stock from there. On reaching there, instead of putting lights on, he waved me towards the window and indicated to a ventilator of a room below of the adjacent house, 'There you can spot a tiger,' he whispered and then directed me in the same low tone, 'You stay back for some more time after everyone leaves.'

We took the fresh stock to the hall and continued our session for some more time before we had our dinner. When everyone left, I stayed back for some more time on the pretext of fixing and configuring his internet modem. And I definitely had a chance to spot the tiger but I will stop here, leaving narration for some other time (as I'm already infamous among bankers after my first book. Some people felt, '....bankers have nothing else to do except indulge in such things.') So I don't want a worse name and therefore, I stop here. Vikas told me that perhaps, the room belonged to the spoilt son of a rich family, and it would not be surprising even if BF was made there.

And oh yes, I had gone to Kanpur to negotiate and finalize the modalities of my niece's marriage. I was entrusted with this responsibility as they thought that I was a better negotiator than anyone else in our family. *Perhaps, this skill sharpened after negotiating very hard with the computer vendors. They say computer vendors are worse than 'aalloo-walas' to deal with.*

Before meeting my niece's prospective in-laws, my mother had cautioned me to negotiate conservatively and start with half the amount from the budgeted one, as mentioned for each item and event in the papers given to me. To be on the safer side, I thought to myself that in some cases I could, and should, quote even lower than that. After all, they were depending on me, and trusted my negotiating skills, and it was time for me to prove that I was a good negotiator. So when it came to call out the amount to be gifted honouring their close relatives, I simply halved the already halved amount as per my mother's instructions. So if it was mentioned as Rs 1100 for somebody in the papers, it was to be quoted as Rs 551 as per my mother's instructions. However, to prove my negotiating skills to my mother, I further halved the amount to Rs 251. Hearing such low amounts, the prospective father-in-law of my niece almost collapsed in the chair. Trying to compose himself, he gestured his wife to come to the other room, 'Sarlaji could you please just come inside for a moment.'

When they came out after fifteen to twenty minutes, he said, 'We have one request to make. These people are very close to us. We won't mind at all even if we are not given anything, or some other items are curtailed. But please raise the amount for these people, if possible, as it is a question of our honour.'

'Your honour is our honour, sir. Absolutely, no problem. How about if the amounts are just doubled (amounts to be quoted originally as per my mother's instructions),' I suggested.

'Oh that would be really great!' he was visibly relieved.

'We may even think about going a step further, if that is

so,' I said as a professional marketing man.

'We will be only too happy, but I would say that is your prerogative,' and the happiness writ large on his face was beyond any description.

16

Life Full of Choppiness

Moving further on my LFC, our next destination after Kanpur was Ahmedabad where my nephew, a Major in the army, was posted. I was keen to visit him, and besides, we had common interest as well. He had told me earlier, over the phone, that he was going to Singapore to purchase some software, for data duplicating and storing and an Indian agent for this software was located at Ahmedabad. Since we were also interested in data storing software at FTMO, and I was working on assessing the efficacy of different real time duplicating and storing software, I wanted to visit this Indian vendor. In fact, my nephew had fixed up my meeting with the vendor, as I was eager to know more about it.

On meeting the vendor when I told him about my purpose of visit and the site (FTMO) for which it was required, he immediately said that somebody had already raised a similar query for some real time mirroring software from the FTMO to his principal at Singapore, and from where it was referred to him. I guessed it must be Rajendran. In our discussion, he clarified that many data duplicating software were available— from low to very high end—from doing basic work of copying data to completely mirroring the primary node and performing very complex functions of mirroring as well as controlling the primary one from some other node. The low-end versions were easily available anywhere in the open market, but the high-end complex ones were not readily available. He further opined that as per the FTMO's requirements, described by me, a medium end version would very well do, though the earlier query raised was for performing very complex functions, requiring a very high-end version.

Though my main purpose of visit to Ahmedabad was to meet that vendor and exchange views about the software with my nephew, but I came to know that now he was not going to Singapore. I could understand his disappointment, but I sensed that there was something more as he was not his usual self. So getting a chance when he was away in his office, I asked his wife, while having evening tea, 'Why does Sunny look so forlorn these days?'

'No...nothing much,' she said as if trying to suppress her feelings.

'Still,' I tried to dig.

'Why did you say that?'

'I sense that he is not his usual self.'

'Oh, yeah... you may be right. But, why does it happen to us only, Chacha?'

'Why? What happened?'

'See, he was doing very well. Perhaps, he was the youngest Major in his core and one of the most qualified, promising and betted candidates for the next promotion. But, first he was dropped from the software purchase team going to Singapore and then bypassed for the next promotion; just because he did not fall in line with the seniors.'

'But following the commands of your seniors is of utmost

importance in defence forces, as far as I understand.'

'Definitely, absolutely no doubt on that count! But how long can you continue to bow down to the unreasonable demands of your seniors?'

'I could not get you?'

'I do not know much, but what I gather from here and there that he became an odd-man-out in the chain of officers clearing inflated bills for local purchases. When he brought this his commandant's notice, he was shocked to know that the he was aware of everything. In fact, he bluntly told him that this was being done as per his directions to bear miscellaneous expenses. He flatly said that he wasn't in a position to do much about it as he had to manage the show when the senior officials and their wives visited the town. He point-blankly told my husband,

> 'Young officer, you are very intelligent and a mature person. I understand your anxiety, but try to understand my position. Tell me how can I manage their five-starred bills when the wives of senior officials visit the station? Naturally, I can't afford from my pocket. So, the money raised through inflated bills goes to that pool from which these shows are managed. Of course, I can't vouch for the few pennies here and there "mis-utilized" by some people, but definitely the major chunk of it goes to that pool and is spent like that.'

> 'But sir, I beg to differ and am afraid that this is not my cup of tea. Sir, you know my dad was also in the army and he had undergone all these phases. Unfortunately, I have not been taught these intricacies

and these are not in my blood. I have seen in my childhood when once how we kids had to pool in money from our savings by breaking our 'gollaks' as my Dad didn't have even that much money in urgency. He had to buy a ticket for his orderly, who was to go home for an emergency. He was so honest, I am told, that at times while travelling in first-class with his colleagues, he didn't have enough money even to afford meals from the dinning-car with other officers. So, he would quietly go to other coach on some pretext or other, and would have ordinary puri-sabzi from the station. Sir, I have been brought up in that environment and with such values.'

'Well, all right Major, if you so insist I can take you off from the purchase and bill clearing process... but I am afraid then you would not be included in the software purchase team going to Singapore. If you still insist, I can discharge you from this responsibility.'

'Sir, I will be highly obliged...'

'Though he was absolved of this responsibility, but naturally it was not liked by them and his report was affected.'

'Oh.'

'Now tell me Chacha what would you call this? Was it the case of disobeying just orders of your seniors or a case of not falling in line with others indulging in unethical practices?'

'No doubt, Sunny did the right thing and we should feel proud of him. Even the question of thinking otherwise should not arise, whatever cost one might have to pay, I feel....These things happen, but he should be satisfied that he did the right thing despite all trials and tribulations.'

'Whatever one may say, still one gets disillusioned by such things.'

'No doubt you feel frustrated when you find that one who is less sincere, less involved and is less knowledgeable than you, is in a far better position than you, only because of his one quality—that is parroting 'yes boss'. It happens everywhere, including in organisations like my bank. Everybody faces such things somewhere down the line in one's career, but one should not get disheartened just because of one event, all part of a game...one has to move on, howsoever a huge drag it may be.'

'Hmm...' It was Sunny. We did not realize when Sunny had come and stood behind us and for how long he was standing there, hearing our conversation.

'Oh, yeah! Life is full of choppiness, full of ups and downs, pleasure, and sorrows. That is what life is! Only thing—one has to flow with life, making the best of it, and enjoying every moment, taking all the highs and the lows in stride.'

◆

In our LFC tour, Nasik was also one of the destinations. While visiting a temple there, we joined a serpentine queue of devotees waiting for a 'darshan.' But the queue was hardly inching forward. I decided to find out why while my wife and son waited. As there was a steel frame, barricading the way for the sanctum of the temple, I had to trace back my way to the entrance side. When I reached the main gate, I asked a guard if there was any possibility of my having the 'darshan'. He looked at me from top to bottom and then quietly pushed me 'in' from the exit side at the gate, 'Pay hundred rupees to this guard while coming out,' he said. As hardly there was any rush on the exit side, I immediately reached the sanctum and had a nice cool 'darshan'. I was surprised that there was such a long queue at the entrance, but hardly was anyone seen coming out at the exit. In fact, they were allowing the people inside the sanctum in a small lot of two-to-three persons, whereas those who reached inside were in no hurry to come out. So, the queue was getting longer and longer. As most of the people inside were back-door entrants like me, security personnel had no moral courage to ask anyone to move out. After having a 'darshan' and finishing it all in no time, I was relaxing in the taxi, when after about an hour or so, my wife and son came out, all tired and frustrated without having a 'darshan' as the queue did not move at all. I didn't tell them that I already had a 'darshan'.

◆

During our trip to Mount Abu, at 'Sunset' point we asked a local whether there was anything else to see beyond the point on that road. He said, 'Yes, at the dead end, you have the "Hanuman" point.' But when we reached there, we did not find any Hanuman temple or idol. When we asked a young couple about 'Hanuman' point, they had a hearty laugh clarifying that what he meant not 'Hanuman' point but 'Honeymoon' point.

17

Adda Revisited

On my return from LFC, I came to know that a demo of real time data duplicating and storing software had already been organized by some other vendor in my absence, as the DFO wanted to do it fast. Perhaps, he was quite worried about the risk involved in working with old servers and so as a precautionary measure, he was very keen to have these systems in place before he retired and relinquished his charge. However, when I told Rajendran about my meeting with one such vendor at Ahmedabad, he denied having contacted any one such there.

I was told that the demo was quite interesting and well attended by the people who had also mitigated their doubts about its use. Being a computer buff and also earlier associated with the selection of the main software, Mr Sikdar took keen interest and participated in the discussions very actively. Later, the vendor was told about the actual requirements of the FTMO in details and shown the main server and associated computers sites of the FTMO.

'Did Rajendran talk to you?' asked Bajpai when I met him on my return.

'No. Why?' I said.

'In fact, he was saying that yes, it was possible to have free, unrestricted internet access on one of the terminals in the server room as Das was suggesting the other day. Rajendran said let the boss come then he would see,' Bajpai said.

'Whattt? Have you told him about BF watching business and all?' I said nervously, completely shocked.

'No buddy, how can I tell him so? Do you think that I am that naive?' asked Bajpai.

'What did you say then?' I asked.

'I asked him generally, if it was possible to have unrestricted internet access from the server room and in case of need if it could be used,' Bajpai said.

'What did he say?' I asked again.

'He said the same thing which I told you just now—yes; it was possible, let the boss come.'

'Okay, but you should have not discussed this with him. Anyway.'

'Okay. I also realized it now, but it happened unwittingly. When I did not see you for quite some time and he happened to come to my department, I unknowingly asked him.'

'It's okay.'

'Now tell us what you think about our proposal?' Bajpai came back to his proposal like the proverbial 'Arjuna's eye'.

'What can I say? You can go there once or twice, but not on a regular basis. So, it won't serve your purpose. Why don't you get BF CDs from the Chandni electronic market at Chowringhee? It is close by,' I said as it was not only risky, but almost impossible to do what they were suggesting. I knew that they would not take my reply in good spirit, but I was helpless.

'But you can't see the same stuff again and again,' Bajpai said bit dejectedly.

'No, you can exchange CDs after deduction of a very nominal amount. This can be done on a regular basis,' I suggested.

'Bugger, the quality of those CDs is very poor, and then who would take care of all these?'

'I can do it, no problem,' I volunteered so as to avoid them at any cost from watching it in the server room, and added in a hush-hush tone, 'I may tell you one more secret source of BF CDs, but this info is strictly for your own personal consumption, not to be passed on.' 'You know Swamy of Admin; he has a very good collection of these, in fact a huge library. You name any country, any region, any language, and he has it. He is crazy. Wherever he visits, his one point programme is to collect BF CDs. Sometimes, he was caught at customs, but got away by offering some CDs to them. Really, great fanatic! I think he is more interested in collecting these than even watching them. What a unique hobby', I said.

'But how do you know all this?' asked Bajpai.

'We stayed together at the guest-house for quite some time. It so happened that both of us joined the office at the same time. He joined from Hyderabad Circle. There he told me about this unusual hobby. Perhaps, these people are more candid to share such things,' I said.

Das joined us with the latest grapevine that Bajpai was being shifted from the Reconciliation Dept to the Cover Dept, swapping places with Mr Sikdar; and some communication regarding purchase of new servers had come from the central office.

On hearing the news of his shifting from Reconciliation Dept to Cover Dept, Bajpai commented, 'It was expected as someone from here was to go to Singapore for reconciliation of some entries, and who would like Bajpai to go? Only blue-eyed like Sikdar could have this privilege.'

Soon, I was called by the DFO.

18

Proposal to Shift

When I met the DFO, he enquired about the progress in hiring servers as a stop gap arrangement until the process of purchasing new ones was completed to replace the existing servers. When I said, 'Not much,' he said, 'I told you to get ready with the alternative plan and work out the details for rental servers. Now see, this letter has arrived saying as the proposal for purchasing new servers is kept in abeyance till further instructions, we should get servers on rentals for the time being.' 'Now, move fast,' he added.

When I told this to Bajpai-Das duo, they told me that there was some murmur at the top, at the central office, to curtail certain operations at Cal, and shift these to Mumbai as a part of rationalizing the foreign operations. Perhaps, this is why they must have decided to keep the proposal for new servers on hold, as the specs of the new ones would now depend on the volume of work here in the future. Meanwhile, I had seriously started scouting for the servers on rentals as replacement for the existing ones.

Within few days of this letter, shelving the tender process for the new servers, it became clear that there was a proposal at the central office to shift certain work from Cal to Mumbai. There was a rumour at the FTMO Cal, that Mumbai being a commercial capital and hub of all financial activities, it was in fact a first step towards ultimately shifting the whole FTMO to Mumbai. A one-day strike for twelve hours from 8:00 am to 8:00 p.m. was announced against this proposed shift.

All leaves were cancelled in view of the strike. The departmental heads were asked to make necessary arrangements for the continuity of the operations on the day of the strike. In fact, some people handling critical operations were identified, and arrangements were made in a nearby hotel at Park Street for their dinner and stay, so that they could come to the office early next morning, on the day of strike. Though these arrangements were made for the concerned officials, some of them managed to accommodate their families with them. We, Rajendran and I, decided to stay back in the office itself that night along with our electrician and the vendor engineer, who was permanently stationed at the FTMO. The vendor engineer's company was informed about it.

By 6:30 in the morning, all the important functionaries reported at the office and were there at their respective desks. The canteen was packed with the food items for the day—from breakfast to dinner. Everything was on the house. Entrance to all the floors, except the ground floor, was locked from inside by 7:30, and entry was restricted. After that only those people, who were not willing to participate in the strike, were allowed to enter the ground floor lobby to mark their presence in the office, but were not allowed to move further to upper floors to avoid risk of any mishap. All arrangements were made for their stay at the ground floor itself. But no one could enter the building after that, being stopped by the striking staff.

We, three of us, Rajendran, our electrician and I, slept

in the office. Bajpai and Das also stayed back. The vendor engineer did not turn up at night, as decided earlier, and was missing in the morning. In fact, while taking a stroll around Park Street, the previous night, after dinner at the hotel, we saw him from behind, walking at a distance with a girl. Around 9 a.m. we got a call from him that he could not make it to the FTMO as he had met with an accident, and now the striking staff was not allowing him to enter the building.

He was stranded outside. When Rajendran heard this, he gestured me to leave him, murmuring, 'Let the bugger doom with them. We will manage; no problem.'

All the essential operations went off unhindered. We managed to keep the systems running throughout the day without any disruption. Though the striking staff could create some disturbances outside the office, at the entrance, but as far as the operations were concerned, the strike was a total failure.

Next day the DFO called me and praised my efforts for keeping all the systems up and running, thus making all the essential operations possible during the strike. 'But you now focus on two things—one, hiring of servers on rentals, and two, drawing of contingency plan covering the preparation of a contingency site as an alternate one to work, in case it is needed,' the DFO expressed his concern in the changed scenario. 'Preparing a contingency site assumes special significance in view of the proposal to shift the office to Mumbai, and possible strikes and shut-downs,' he emphasized.

19

The Nexus

'Rajendran, have you seen this circular in today's email? They have selected and identified two officials for software training in the US, and both are from the central office Mumbai. One of them, the female officer, is your batch mate. Is she eligible to be considered?' I asked Rajendran after seeing the email.

'Yes, I know, sir. I talked to her yesterday. As I told you sir, when names were asked, both of us were not eligible, as we had not cleared the certification examination conducted by the software company, the main requirement for this training. But during the three days' time, given for sending recommendations, she cleared the exam!'

'Very smart! However, is it possible to clear the exam in three days?' I was surprised.

'Technically, one can—as everything is online—register for the exam online by paying the fee through credit card; select one of the test centres of the online testing bodies; select the date and any available two-hour slot on that date. Then he has to reach the centre, write the test online, and get the scores immediately, then and there on the screen, after finishing the test. They also send the scores directly to the designated authority, indicated by the candidate in the registration form, within twenty four hours, by email. So, if one registers tonight for the exam, he can take the test tomorrow morning and have the scores sent by next day to the competent authority. It can be done in a day.' 'But don't you think that some preparation is also required before the test even if it is online, howsoever intelligent you may be?' I expressed my doubts.

'Yes, there is a catch. I am told that there are people specializing in writing these tests, who can help you in the test at the centres for a price. Since it is online and one has to be very fast to score the passing percentile, at times they themselves sit on the terminal, instead of directing the candidate. It all depends on the test centre in-charge.'

'Amazing! But are these people not caught and the centres are not blacklisted?'

'They are all hand in glove. It is business—from IT certification MNCs to test conducting bodies, to their franchisees, to test taking candidates. See, an officer clearing this exam in our bank, besides being reimbursed for full examination fee, gets an honorarium of Rs. 20,000 from the bank. So, he doesn't mind passing a share of this booty to the exam-writer. Centres thus get more and more candidates by allowing them to cheat. IT certification MNCs, fully aware of all this, ignore it as their only interest has in selling their products, and this way their products and services become popular very fast as the number of people clearing their exam increases, the number of those using their products also goes up. The only thing they must do is to create an aura and hype for a particular exam.'

'Great, what a superb commercial alliance!'

20

Cherian Speaks

I was feeling a bit low and indifferent. Bajpai and Das were also not there. Bajpai had gone out on some official work to the central office whereas Das had gone to Bhubaneswar on some personal work. I did not know what to do. Feeling bored, I just opened my emails. And lo! There was an email from my ex-FBI batchmate Cherian. What a pleasant surprise it was!

Cherian was my batchmate and had started his career with me as a probationer at FBI. After my few years at the FBI, we again had a chance to come quite close when we both headed branches at the same Gorakhpur zone of Lucknow Circle. I was posted at the Petrochemical Complex branch and Cherian was posted at the Azamgarh one.

While posted at Azamgarh, Cherian unearthed a bungling by a staff member involving a large sum. But as luck would have it, the case boomeranged when the accused staff member committed suicide and Cherian was named as an abettor of the suicide in the FIR, landing him behind the bars.

Cherian, though later completely absolved of his role in the suicide case, and his stand against the erring staff member totally vindicated, chose to resign from the FBI after the unfortunate episode. As I was supporting Cherian in the case and stood by him all along in his fight against the guilty, I also was entangled in the office politics. In the process, I became a centre of fury of various warring lobbies. This resulted in my own transfer, quite disgracefully, from Gorakhpur.

We exchanged a few emails until he was at his native place at Kottayam in Kerala, and then I got engrossed in my own affairs. Later, when I tried to contact him through emails, they bounced. Perhaps, he had deactivated his last email-id known to me. Last, he was heard to be somewhere in Europe.

And now an email–

Dear Rajesh,

Long time no see. Hope, everything is fine. I am sorry that I could not contact you earlier as I was engrossed in my new roles and new phase of life. You might know that after cooling my heels for some time at Kottayam, after leaving the bank, I landed in Europe. Soon, I shifted to the US, where I also did a diploma in computers applications. Now, I am working for a finance software company based in Chicago, though mostly on move between Europe and the US.

As you know, long back, for some time my family had stayed in Kanpur and had developed some acquaintances there. I happened to get in touch with one of them, today. He mentioned about Kanpur in the context of some tussle going on in two warring churches of northern India. The very name of Kanpur immediately reminded me of you and then I looked for your last email-id, which luckily I found. Therefore, the email.

I am sorry that because of me, you had to suffer

too. I trust, things are under control and comfortable. I have no regrets. It is all part of the game called life. I have the satisfaction that I did what I thought was right. Ultimately, my stand was vindicated. Whatever others may think, we are the winners!

Please do write about yourself and take care.

Cherian.

I immediately emailed back–

Dear Cherian,

What a pleasant surprise to receive your email! The joy simply cannot be described in words. I tried a number of times to contact you on the old email id I had, but the email bounced every time. Here, things are as usual. Do not feel that I had to suffer because of you. Nobody suffers because of anybody else, but because of his own doings. Everyone has to go through the same situation, which he creates for others.

I feel proud of the way you stood firm against all odds. Despite all trials and tribulations that you had been through, you remained undaunted in the face of adversity. Yes, you are right, we are true winners, and I am proud that I stood by you.

As you know that after you left Azamgarh for Kottayam, I was also unceremoniously transferred from the Petrochemical branch, Gorakhpur. Out of disgust, I had gone on a long leave in protest. After two or three quick transfers, consequence to my continued tiff with the circle management, and a long leave in between, now I have landed in Cal in the Computers Group of the FTMO and as of now, I am reasonably settled. Let us see, if I also follow your footsteps, leaving FBI. So, that's it.

How about you, how are you finding your new job and life there as an NRI?

Keep in touch Cherian, and take care,

Rajesh.

P.S. Can we chat?

Cherian responded–

Hello Rajesh,

Oh, I also feel like chatting with you. It has been long since we had a 'bull session'. How about chatting at 11.30 pm IST today? Hope that would suit you, as these days I'm in London.

Till then,
Cherian.

And we carried on our chat at the night–

Me: Hi Cherian, welcome on chat after such a long time. So naturally, I would like to share and exchange many things. But, first thing first. Yes, I was asking you about your job there.

Cherian: As I wrote to you, I am working with a finance software company based in Chicago. They develop wide-ranging software in the financial areas and then customize these as per the clients' requirements. Presently, I am associated with the group working on linking software for two computer terminals or two different computer networks. Since you are a computer man yourself, you can understand these things well. I understand you must also be working with these things.

Me: Great. Yes, our operations at the FTMO are fully computerized and networked. Does this linking software just transfer the data from one port to other after linking them or does it do something more?

Cherian: Until now, it was just linking two ports for data transfer only. But now we have improved it to mirror one port from another in real time, as per the client's requirement. In fact, I am in London to check this out, at a client's site.

Me: Interesting, would love to work with it. Can you control primary terminal from the mirroring terminal?

Cherian: Well, this software can do mirroring for limited purposes and that too between two ports only. It is also supposed to control one terminal's functioning from another, but again, in a restricted sense.

Me: Oh, I see. But it does mirroring as well as controlling, though in the limited sense.

Cherian: Yes. In fact, today we tried mirroring at a client's site and it worked perfectly. 'Controlling', we will try tomorrow, and then only it can be confirmed that it works for it too.

Me: Good. Wish you all the best for tomorrow's trial. Hope, there won't be any hitches.

Cherian: I hope so too. Let us see.

Me: And now the next part of my query—how do you find life there?

Cherian: Life is very different here. No doubt, that the average standard of living is very high, especially in USA. But then life is very hectic and mechanical. It is very fast and there is no personal touch. Though everybody, known or unknown will smile at you without fail, but its all too mechanical. They seem to have no or less feelings and are not attached to anything. That is why they perhaps, do not hesitate at all, to change jobs, places, etc., and also their partners. Everything is weighed in terms of money, wealth, and convenience.

Me: And the daily chores of life,vis-à-vis that in India?

Cherian: One big difference, which I find here in comparison to India, is that here everything is automatic and done as per norms, whereas in India for each thing, small or big, you have to strive. Here it is either done or it won't be done, there is no middle course. This perhaps, makes life much simpler here.

Me: You may be right but I feel that in India, in some way or other, we ourselves are responsible for this state of affairs. We talk so much about being straight but many a times fall prey to double standards, and indulge in unethical practices, promoting wrong interests and thus perpetuating this culture. This may be out of social pressures or status consciousness or simply out of over enthusiasm. See, what Shyamlal has done, if you remember him.

Cherian: Yes-yes, I remember him very well. The same guy for whom we did some manipulations in the promotion test?

Me: Yes, the same person. You must remember how we corrected his answers in his answer sheet while we were checking copies as examiners for the promotional test in the centralized evaluation cell at the Circle Head Office.

Cherian: Yes, you told me that he had worked under you at one of your earlier branches. He made some special symbol, perhaps 'Om' or 'Swastik', on the first page for identification of his answer sheet.

Me: Exactly. And what luck he had when later, after qualifying in the written test, his name figured in my zones interview board. Being ES there, it was a cakewalk for Shyamlal to clear the interview as well.

Cherian: Yes, I remember you telling me that he was ultimately promoted. But, where is he now?

Me: Now the bugger is behind the bars on charges of defrauding the bank of huge sums. In fact, from my branch days itself I felt that he was not above board, but still to show my powers and reach, I helped him out of the way, when he approached me. So who is responsible? We are.

Cherian: True...

Me: How is life as an NRI?

Cherian: For NRIs life is more difficult as on one hand they carry a heavy load of their Indian values and traditions, and on the other, they have to strive harder to prove that they are far better off and comfortable there than they would have been in their own country. So, for them, it is not only more mechanical but also very stressful as they continuously live under internal conflicts and dilemmas. They are very often torn between the lifestyle there and the traditions back home.

Me: So the best thing for them would be to totally merge and adopt that culture.

Cherian: Of course, for the second generation migrant it is easier. And they not only do it but at times, they overdo it out of enthusiasm, just to show and prove that they are more Americans than the Americans themselves. But this is just not possible for the first generation migrant for two reasons—firstly, all said and done, whatever you say, you are not totally accepted as a part of them, and which, in any case you are not; secondly, you are not able to sever your connections with your roots in India. So, you are always under pressure to show your worth to people back at home, and as a result, you never live your own life.

Me: Yes, this divided loyalty is very painful. I fail to understand why they live there on transitional basis. Why they want to do small household things like stitching and house furnishing from India and carry all the way? Is it not funny to do such things saving few dollars here and there, as these things are little cheaper in India? Also, what is the need to get second grade items of odd sizes from there, for relatives and acquaintances in India? Of course, earlier we were crazy about such things, but now everything is available here, and perhaps of better quality, and certainly better than those second grade items there. People here now realize that it is better to buy things here itself, of their choices, sizes and requirements; and of course, which now they can afford because of better purchasing powers.

Cherian: In fact, to a certain extent, their relatives in India are also responsible for NRIs not adopting the lifestyle there completely as they keep directing them from India, and that too, from their own point of views and in the Indian context.

Me: Exactly. See, for some days, there has been tension brewing in my extended family over my nephew in the US who switched from an MNC to a start-up. They are green-card holders there. Of course, it is nothing unusual there, and a routinely thing, but here, we with middle-class mentality, are feeling very uncomfortable, and are greatly worried.

Cherian: Even in India, this concept of changing jobs is catching up fast.

Me: Still, we middle-class people feel more comfortable with the secured, structured type of environment, obviously at the cost of growth and progress.

Cherian: Yes, true. I think let us stop here as it must be too late in India. Tomorrow, I will still be in London, so we can chat again at the same time, 11.30 p.m. IST. And I have to tell you the results of the 'controlling' trial also. Till then, bye.

Me: Okay. Bye-bye, take care.

Next day, we continued our chat.

Cherian: Hi Rajesh!

Me: Hi!

Cherian: Firstly, I must tell you that the 'controlling' trial was successful. We could control one port from another port as desired.

Me: So it worked! Great! Congratulations.

Cherian: Yes...Of course, in a limited sense, as I told you. But for client's purposes, we could control one terminal from another. Now I can say with certainty that the software works for 'mirroring' as well as 'controlling'. So, my job here is done and now I will be flying back to the US tomorrow, early in the morning.

Me: Good. I am so excited that I want to see myself how it works.

Cherian: Well, let me see if I can send you, the 'limited version-feel-yourself' copy from there. Of course, it would give you just the feel of the software and of its functions. It will be without security checks, so you should not run it on actual business systems. Needless to say, it will be your personal copy for your own personal use.

Me: Superb. Thanks a lot buddy. I will eagerly wait for it. *All the while, I had in my mind of trying Das's idea of linking monitoring terminal to some outside terminal with this software.*

Cherian: You won't have to wait for it. I will email it tomorrow itself—different components separately. Though of very limited capability, still the software code would be a little heavy and will take time in downloading. I will email the installation manual and the key separately. Hope, for a person like you, it won't be a problem to install and have a feel of it.

Me: Let me see.

Cherian: No, it won't be a problem. Moreover, it is a 'do-it-yourself' kit.

Me: Oh, ya!

Cherian: Okay. By the way, the other day you said something that you also wanted to fall in line with me. Are you, by any chance, planning to leave FBI??

Me: I had been contemplating for long, but I wanted to leave on a positive note and was waiting for the opportune time. Now, I feel I am approaching that moment.

Cherian: What do you mean by 'opportune time'?

Me: By 'opportune time' I mean when everything is justified, at the right time, as the priorities in a person's life keep changing. One may have a lifetime dream, but he can defer it for a more opportune time, when he becomes relatively free from other obligations of life. So that it is an 'opportune time' to realize his lifetime dream.

Cherian: Okay. Before closing the session, tell me how is your wife Meenakshi and her college?

Me: She is fine. But in her college, the management is

caught between the two warring churches.

Cherian: I know: the whole tussle must be to get hold of innumerable huge properties left behind by the British. The best solution, I feel, would be to make a law that these should be used only for church and educational institutions, for which these are meant, and nobody should be able to dispose of these properties. Say my hello and best wishes to Meenakshi. I take leave now. Do make a plan to visit the US.

Me: Oh yes, let us make our passports first.

Cherian: Great! You still don't have one. I can't believe it... Now I understand why you were so critical of NRIs, being sour grapes for you...Bye-bye. Take care until we interact again.

Me: Bye-bye.

Next day, Cherian, as promised, e-mailed me the different components of the software along with the installation manual and the key.

21

Playing with Fire

'Oh you handled the situation very well during the strike, people were telling me, at the central office,' Bajpai echoed their appreciation of my efforts in keeping all the systems up, and thus running the essential operations during the one day strike. He had just come back from his visit to the central office.

'But at the same time, I say you have now earned more enemies than ever. People were already after you for taking so many pangas as you have provoked them number of times—blocking their sites, not obliging them with few PCs for their union meet and teasing them with your other small actions now and then, and now this,' commented Das.

'So what; I only carry out my duties, nothing more. Yes, of course conscientiously. Even then, if anybody gets antagonized, it is not my problem. It is his. I hardly care for anything else except my job. Moreover, you can't satisfy all people at all times as per their whims and fancies,' I reacted a little sharply.

'Bugger, what he wants to say is that you should do your job all right, but avoid hurting sentiments of others so openly and blatantly. Do things quietly, as far as possible, without confronting others,' Bajpai intervened.

'Yes exactly, that's what,' Das endorsed Bajpai.

'Okay, but it is very difficult to change one's basic nature.

Anyway, I will definitely try to keep your advice in mind,' I said.

'Leave this, and now tell us when you are going to fulfil your promise. Otherwise, also, it calls for some celebrations. So when,' Bajpai demanded.'Yes-yes,' Das also echoed with Bajpai.

'Bugger, at least show us the server room if nothing more, though you yourself said that we could go there once or twice,' Bajpai reminded me of my promise, when I kept mum.

'It is very risky, I say. It's not a kid's play. I then just said that you could see the room,' I reiterated my reluctance.

'Okay, then let us have a feel of the room at least,' Bajpai insisted.

'Okay, tomorrow is Saturday and it is a half day. Both of you stay back in your department after office hours. I will give you a call, then you come to my cabin, and we will go there. But all very quietly, I don't want to make it public,' I said. But I had something else in my mind. In fact, I wanted to try the 'mirroring and controlling' software kit sent by Cherian.

'Why should we be so secretive, we can anyway have a look,' Das said.

'See, in the first place, entry is highly restricted because it is very critical to the operations at the FTMO. Secondly, when the two of you go there, people will get curious and suspicious. Moreover, you are not going to come out immediately. That is why I don't want people to take note of it unnecessarily,' I clarified my position.

'Okay,' both said in unison.

'It's better if no one should have any inkling to it. You see, you are not going to just have a look. You are going to sit there for some time, and the server room has no arrangement of bolting the door from inside except that lock. This sensor lock anyway can be opened from outside by the authorised person even if it has been locked from inside. Apart from me, the DFO, Admin. (Security Officer) and Rajendran have the authorized key (password) to it, and these people can anytime open it and enter unannounced,' I warned them in advance.

'Oh-ho, very high-tech,' said Das.

'And risky if...' added Bajpai little worriedly.

'That is why I had been keeping quiet all along about this. It is not advisable to be around the room very often,' I cautioned them.

'How about the senior vendor engineer? He at least must have access,' said Bajpai.

'Nope, no way.'

'That means not even the senior vendor engineer can enter without you people,' Das was surprised.

'Yup, only four of us have keys, no one else,' I clarified.

Next day when I called Bajpai in the morning, he was little shaky, 'Boss, I think let us drop the idea.'

'Why, what happened?' I asked.

'No, nothing. Is not it too risky? I don't think it is worth taking so much risk. We just wanted to have some fun, but if it leads to so much tension, then what is the point? So, leave it,' better sense prevailed over Bajpai.

'Yes, we must maintain its sanctity as it is very critical. Anyway, you come to my cabin in the afternoon, when I give you a call as I may try something else,' I said.

When they came in the afternoon after everybody had left the department, I told them that I would try to link and mirror my terminal outside with the particular terminal inside the server room so that they could access any site from my terminal as well. They were amazed that it was really possible. 'Yes, as the idea given earlier by Das, it can be done, but I will have to juggle a little, and the terminal inside will not do its monitoring function as long as it remains linked to my terminal.'

'Will this not affect main functioning of the system?' Bajpai's face was again contoured.

'In fact, that is not a problem as monitoring functions would be passed on to my terminal for that period. Anyway, no monitoring as such is required now. But the real issues are linking and then de-linking later, and to do all this I will have to enter the server room.'

'What is so great about it? You, anyway, keep going and coming out all through the day,' Das was puzzled.

'That is not the issue. I don't want this entry to be recorded,' I said.

'Recorded? What do you mean?' Bajpai was alarmed again.

'Oh, I haven't told you one of the secrets of the server room. It has hidden cameras which keep recording every activity inside room, apart from the sensor door lock which maintains a log of door movement,' I said in a guarded tone.

'Oh gosh!' they wailed in unison.

'No problem, I will switch the recording off, for the time being,' I said, as now it was a question of my reputation. Moreover, I was eager and excited to do something different— link the two terminals with the help of the software kit sent by Cherian. Grown-up yet not so grown-up. . . to resist the excitement of something new and different.

'You see, with so many checks and hassles involved in it we need not carry out our plan,' Das said little worriedly.

'I say it is not required at all. Leave it,' said Bajpai anxiously.

'In fact, anyway, I wanted to experiment with this linking of my terminal, for long' and I darted towards server room door before they could react or say anything, gesturing them to sit there. Before entering the room, I switched off the recording and went straight to the terminal. The software was already loaded there. I changed some settings there, and came out to my terminal. There again, I changed certain settings, synchronizing it with the internet protocol address of the terminal inside. Lo! It started functioning. It was completely linked and started mirroring the inside terminal. I screeched, 'Hurray!' in a muffled tone mocking a punch in the air. Bajpai and Das, who were all the while sitting breathless across the table, also came around me leaping from their chairs. I showed them that now it was accessing any site and passed the terminal keyboard to them. Das tried to access some site, and it worked. Then Bajpai tried some other site, and it switched to that site. Excited, Das pulled the keyboard and said, 'Let me try one porn site,' and keyed in its address. But, no sooner than it switched to porn site, Bajpai pulled the keyboard back and keyed in a new site, 'First watch this exclusive Aarti (porn site)' and waited it to switchover to a new site. When it did not happen, he again keyed in the address of the new site, but in vain. In fact, it was not taking any new address and sticking to the porn site entered by Das. We exited the internet connection and again opened the browser. As soon as it opened, it again automatically went to the same porn site. 'Oh shit!' I cried. 'What is happening? Has it hung?' They were completely perplexed, but it was clear to me that it had become the permanent default site, as had happened earlier with the DFO's terminal. So, I immediately decided to stop trying any further and to get the systems to their original status first. 'Any problem?' asked Bajpai gravely seeing me tense. 'We will have to revert to the original status. Let us see if we can?' I said little unsure. I immediately exited the internet and de-linked my terminal resetting it to its original configuration. Now my terminal returned to its original state and ceased to have unrestricted access to the internet. I went inside the server room and reset the monitoring terminal to its original configuration too, uninstalling the software. It was working otherwise all right, but whenever we tried to start internet, it would automatically be going to that porn site. Now that porn site had become the permanent, default site on this terminal. In fact, my terminal, when linked, was mirroring this terminal only and so the problem was with this terminal. I tried my level best to undo this but could not succeed. I knew from my earlier experience of the DFO's terminal that only solution would to change the terminal altogether. So, I decided to leave situation that day as it was, and change the terminal on Monday. 'We will have to leave at this stage today and change the terminal on Monday,' I told them as all along they were watching me struggling in silence. Though we were totally shaken by this unexpected glitch, but the great solace was that all other functions were working normally. The anxiety and apprehensions were writ large on our faces. Bajpai and Das were more unnerved than I was, as they felt that they were responsible for what was happening. Moreover, they felt that they were not authorized to be there. They, then and there, wanted to discuss the possible consequences and the strategy to face the crisis. But I advised them to leave the place first, 'First and foremost, we should move out from here, lest anyone notices us.'

'Oh yes,' they said and immediately got up.

'You two go first, I will follow you. Wait for me at Haldiram's,' I instructed. They rushed out, without looking back.

When I reached Haldiram's, a short distance from our office, they were waiting outside, smoking, inhaling as hard as possible, to calm their nerves. While discussing various options over cups of tea at Haldiram's, they were of the opinion that whatever was to be done should be done on Sunday itself, and felt that I should call Rajendran for help. But I firmly believed that neither should we be there on Sunday nor should we involve Rajendran at any cost, as it would expose us. 'Let him notice it in due course and handle the situation on his own, when he comes in on Monday. He anyway comes before me. Don't worry, I will tackle this, but none of us should ever talk about this incident. In fact, not even talk about it amongst ourselves. And remember this, no one should ever know that you two were with me on this Saturday afternoon,' I warned them. 'So, coming on Sunday is automatically ruled out. Why should we invite others' attention unnecessarily by coming on Sunday,' I added. We resolved to act on those lines and dispersed.

When I reached office on Monday morning, Rajendran rushed to me on seeing me, 'Sir, when I came to the office this morning, the recording of the server room was off.'

Oh I forgot to put it back on, I was about to say, but stopped myself in time. In fact, in the rush of the unexpected incidents on Saturday, I had forgotten to switch on the recording after leaving the server room. It was a blunder but nothing could be done now. Taking control of the situation immediately, I pretended to be taken by total surprise, 'What! How come? Put it back on. Must have happened due to some electrical surge or spike.'

'I have already put it on,' informed Rajendran.

'And immediately call its AMC vendor to check it,' I instructed Rajendran.

'Yes sir... And one more thing sir, the monitoring terminal is behaving like the DFO terminal once did—it is automatically opening up and sticking to one particular site if you access the internet,' informed Rajendran.

'Ohho. Did you try to reset it?' I asked.

'Yes, I have tried everything whatever I could, but nothing is happening...I think now we will have to replace the terminal, as was done with the DFO's one. Nothing else would work,' and as Rajendran was telling me this, my intercom rang. It was a call from the DFO secretariat informing that one senior functionary from the central office had come and would, in all possibility, visit the server room. I told Rajendran about this development and asked him to immediately replace that terminal.

'But sir, we do not have such high end terminal readily available with us. Moreover, it will take time to configure the new one even if it is made available,' Rajendran expressed his doubts.

'Then...? You do one thing. Replace the fuse of the terminal's display-monitor by a blown-off fuse immediately, so that it would look as if the fuse has blown just now. This way it will stop displaying anything, including any site, but will continue all its functions silently,' I spontaneously suggested. The idea occurred to me in a flash, and later, even I could not believe that I had suggested it.

After the visit, which went off smoothly, I asked Rajendran, 'You didn't tell me what site it was.'

'Oh it was a similar site like the one, which had got stuck on the DFO's terminal,' Rajendran said bit mischievously.

'Oh that means the DFO must have come here in our absence,' I also responded in the same spirit in lighter vein, and both of us had a hearty laugh.

'But now you must find some suitable terminal as fast as possible for replacing this one. You check your inventory and identify some high-end terminal with similar specs, and which could be taken off from there and shifted here easily without much disturbance,' I directed Rajendran. I felt that the sudden visit by the senior official was godsend as our attention was diverted by his visit, and it saved me the embarrassment of checking the terminal with Rajendran. Moreover, now I also remembered that the terminal had its own webcam, which might have recorded me fiddling around, on Saturday. But with the impromptu action of turning the display off, the chances of somebody watching that recording were also over. Though I played with the fire by juggling around in the server room but the providence was with me so nothing untoward happened, and I was saved a lot of embarrassing consequences.

In the meanwhile, the recording system AMC vendor had also come and checked it. 'But I don't find any fault. I do not know why it went off when every module is functioning perfectly,' the engineer expressed his helplessness in detecting any cause for it going off.

'It could be because of some momentary electrical surge (a sudden large voltage for very short duration), which might have passed undetected through its electrical filter, turning it off,' I suggested.

'Yes-yes, you are very right, sir. This must be the reason,' he said with a 'Eureka' expression on his face and gave his report to this effect. Next day, I sent my detailed report about the recording system turning off along with the AMC engineers report to the DFO, for information.

I emailed Cherian also about the software-

Dear Cherian,

Thank you for sending the software. I tried it and did work very well. Something new and great was experienced! Played some tricks and did some mischief as well.

Keep it up. Thanks.
Rajesh.

22

And Got Me

'Rajesh, I'm sorry to serve you with an "explanation letter" received from Lucknow circle. I think it is asking for an explanation about a car loan case during one of your earlier postings,' the DFO said in a grim voice, handing a sealed envelope to me. And ultimately, they got me. My detractors at Lucknow were ever since trying very hard to embroil me in some case to fix me up. They were searching for documents at various places of my earlier postings to find out something against me at the behest of a senior circle functionary, who was to retire in few months' time. And finally, they dug up a case in one of my previous postings, where they could find a lapse. As I came out of the DFO's office, I felt a lot of eyes following, and could hear the murmurs behind me. Some people in the corridor crossed me heads down, instead of looking at me with usual smiles or greetings, as if I was declared some offender. Though the matter was supposed to be confidential, it seemed it was already public.

It was such a setup that for some reason or the other if you had fallen out of grace or favours of your boss, you would be treated like a pariah, an outcast, and would be ostracized by all others without knowing the reason. People would shun you and not dare to come near you, or see eye to eye with you lest they were noticed. You would be avoided, as if you had contracted some infectious disease. You would be totally isolated and ignored.

The case was related to my posting at Petrochemical Complex Branch, near Gorakhpur. As we were the only bank located inside their campus, we catered to their personal banking needs, apart from carrying out big deals with the company. We had a MOU (memorandum of understanding) with the company that whatever personal loans such as car, housing, etc., their employees availed of from the bank, the company would be responsible for payment of such loans after deducting instalments from their salaries. Even if for some reason, the employee ceased to be employed by the company, it was the company's responsibility to deduct the remaining loan, outstanding from his terminal benefits. So as such, our loans to their employees were absolutely secured and there was no risk at all involved. Even then, we used to complete all the required formalities. However, in one stray car loan case, it so happened that the concerned borrower employee, who was sanctioned a car loan very recently, under bizarre personal circumstances, had to leave the place at once, before the car could be registered at the Gorakhpur RTO (Regional Transport Office) and bank's hypothecation could be registered.

It was a really unusual case. The employee was a young engineer from Kerala and had married about a year ago. As it was a petrochemical plant, it ran on 24 × 365 days basis and worked on three shifts. Every employee had to undergo shift rotation. The plant was located in an isolated remote place and the housing colony was further away at about 5 kilometres from the plant, keeping the potential safety hazards of a gas plant in mind. As there was no habitation and related public amenities including public transport, company buses plied between plant and housing colony at office hours. Employees mostly commuted by the company bus, barring few occasions when they wanted to drive their own cars, if they had one. It was required to keep their vehicles in running condition as there was no other occasion to drive their cars, with everything being confined to the campus. This man was also commuting by bus until he bought a new car. It was the second day since he had brought the car from Gorakhpur. When his dream of owning a car came true, he wanted to distribute sweets at his department as well at the bank. So, he decided to travel by car that day. Moreover, he wanted to complete the RTO forms also and have them signed by the bank. But when he landed at the branch, he found that he had forgotten to bring some papers from home. Since the RTO registration should be done right after the delivery of the vehicle, he decided to get those missing papers immediately from his home and he left for these. On reaching, he found the milkman's bicycle standing outside the house, but the doors were bolted from inside. Somehow, he decided to enter his house from the roof. So, he got in touch with his neighbour, who happened to be on a night shift that day. He entered his house from the roof by jumping from the neighbour's adjoining rooftop. When he reached his bedroom window he could not believe his eyes. His wife was lying in a compromising position in the milkman's arms.

He did not know what to do. His friends advised that to avoid further embarrassment, he should at once leave the campus. So he told the Head HR of the company over the phone, narrating the whole incident, and left Gorakhpur with his wife, never to return to the campus. It was surprising that his wife did not know Hindi at all, and the milkman could not speak even proper Hindi, leave alone English or Malayalam. In fact, the engineer had been suspicious about his wife's behaviour for a long time, but had had no means to come home from the plant during office hours. So as soon as he got a car, he decided to check in during office hours by pretending to get the missing RTO papers. It was rumoured that she had sexual relationships with the neighbour, who never had the same shift as her husband. Later, when the milkman caught her fancy, this neighbour passed on the information to the engineer about what was going on in his house in his absence. The engineer, as a special case, was immediately transferred, to the Chennai plant, and all his household items, including the new unregistered car was transported alongside by the company. The car was later registered with the Chennai RTO and so the bank's hypothecation with the RTO could not be registered.

As the instalments continued to come regularly, I did not bother about the RTO registration. When I spoke to their Head HR about it, he said, 'Why do you bother? You have MOU with us, so it is our responsibility to liquidate the loan. Wherever he is posted, you will get the instalments on time. If for some reason he leaves the company, your loan will be liquidated from his terminal benefits.'

On leaving the DFO's office, I told Bajpai about the letter. He immediately said, 'If you remember, I told you sometime back, based on these bastards' inside info that people at the

Lucknow Circle were working overtime to fix you up and soon you would be nailed down.'

'Oh yes,' and then I narrated whole case to him.

'Great! Now you will have a paid Kanpur trip on the pretext of going to Lucknow, for perusing the case. Don't worry. *Woh isme koi jhat nahi ukhar sakte hain*. They can't do a damn,' Bajpai said coolly. He further asked, 'Any idea, what is the position of the account now?'

'Yes only last month, one guy came from the branch for the reconciliation of the outstanding branch's NOSTRO entries (transactions done in foreign currencies at our branch). He said that the account was running perfectly regular and was about to be liquidated, as only very few instalments remained to be paid,' I said.

'Ch…ch…ch…you poor guy. You have all my sympathies. You will now get very few chances for paid Kanpur trips,' bantered Bajpai.

23

The Ultimate

It was Friday evening, and I had just come back from Bajpai's department after chatting and seeing him off, as he was leaving for vacations that evening, availing LFC. So, I had gone to say 'happy holidays' to him. His predecessor, Mr Sikdar, who was head there, prior to Bajpai, had also come there to say boodbye. Das was away, busy with his son's admissions. As there was nothing urgent or pressing, I decided to call it a day. Rajendran had already left in the afternoon. He was going for a job interview in some other bank at a higher level. Ever since he got overlooked for the training in the US, he had decided to leave the bank and was trying elsewhere for a higher position.

I looked at my watch; it was half past six. It was not that early, and I thought I could leave office. I was about to get up, when I heard some footsteps in the corridor. Before I could make out who it was, I saw the DFO, followed by a few people, rushing towards my cabin. It was no time to expect the DFO there, and that too totally unannounced. He visibly looked agitated. Jumping out of my chair at once, I rushed out to receive him. He immediately asked me, 'Where is Rajendran?'

'Sir, he has already left.'

'Then who is inside the server room? Who has entered the server room with Rajendran's key?'

'Server room? No one sir. It's not possible.'

'But I saw someone inside the room through the recorder. In fact, perhaps two. Come, hurry up, and open the door of the room.'

As soon as I opened the door with my key, we could not believe our eyes. The vendor engineer, permanently stationed at the FTMO, was embracing some girl. They immediately wriggled out of each other's arms, tidying their clothes. Before we could understand anything, the girl darted out of the door, followed by the engineer, and they started running towards the staircase. We ran after them too, but before we could catch them, we heard a loud thump. We reached the staircase, but there was no sign of them. When we looked down from the balcony, we saw some commotion there and people gathered around the cars parked there. As it was already dark, we could not make out much from the nineteenth floor. We rushed to the lifts to reach the ground floor, as fast as possible. There lay the girl's body on one of the cars' roof, parked there.

Everything happened so fast that we were totally taken aback. We did not know what to do. We were completely shocked. Suddenly, I realized the gravity of the situation. I immediately gestured the DFO to leave the site and indicated his personal secretary to escort him. Soon, police arrived from the adjacent police station and took the body in its possession. Meanwhile, I tried to search for the vendor engineer, but there was absolutely no sign of him. In fact, I combed whole parking area, and also around it, if by any chance....I asked the security people to check the staircase from the nineteenth floor to the ground floor, but apparently he was nowhere. I gestured to the Security Officer and the Liaison Officer to one side and whispered to them that there was no need to tell the police about their presence in the server room. Moreover, the vendor engineer was missing, so we could just say that she was alone.

Meanwhile, on coming to know about the incident, some other senior officers, close confidants of the DFO, also arrived. They advised the DFO to not associate the FTMO's name at all with the incident. We were immediately huddled into the DFO's chamber, and it was decided to keep the FTMO out of the case—a girl somehow had sneaked into the building and jumped from the nineteenth floor, committing suicide. Only thing, it was a security lapse, and that too on the part of a security personnel of an external security agency. The story was to be painted such to the police, but then our Security Officer informed us that he had already recorded the FIR. So it was decided to immediately avail of the services of the Liaison Officer and Security Officer along with a local official who had good connections in the police department, to change the FIR. I was asked to remove the recording stick (pen-drive type memory stick) from the recording system immediately.

Before removing the recording stick, I copied its data until before the last three days on a new blank stick and replaced it with that newly-copied stick. I not only changed the recording stick with a new one but also rendered the recording system non- functional by smashing some connections inside the console (main unit of any system or machine), making it look like as if it had stopped functioning three days ago.

Everybody was asking the same question. How did they enter the server room with Rajendran's key? How did they get the key? Did Rajendran give it himself? Was it given to the vendor engineer for some work? Did Rajendran have some ulterior motives? All these questions were troubling me too. However, I had no doubt about Rajendran's integrity, still... But why would he take such suicidal risk with his key? *No-no, it was not possible.*

We left the office around 11.30 or so. Next day, newspapers carried a news item—'A girl committed suicide after sneaking into a Maidan skyscraper'. There was no mention of FTMO in the news item, and it included only the building's name.

Next day I reached office a little early. Anyway, I had to be there early as Rajendran was on leave. The first thing I did after reaching, was to call the recording system AMC vendor and fired him for not attending to the system despite the complaint being lodged three or four days ago. 'But sorry sir, I have never been told about it. I'm hearing about this from you for the first time. Of course, for the last two days I was not here,' he said apologetically.

'Oh, nobody told you about it, not even Rajendran? Anyway, today he is on leave. I will ask him once he returns,' I pretended. 'Maybe its a communication gap as you were away. Anyway, you attend to it right away. And mind you, it is Saturday today, so its a half-day working only,' I again bullied him.

Soon, he arrived to attend to the system and set it right in no time as I indirectly indicated the source of the fault. He submitted his report and left. I heaved a great sigh of relief, as now the story was complete. Now it could be authentically said that the system was down for the last three to four days and had been repaired today. And consequently, there was no recording for the last three to four days.

So far so good, but one question, apart from their

mysterious entry into the server room, was constantly bugging me since the last day was, how did the DFO come to know about somebody's presence in the server room? Normally, he would be too busy to watch, live or recorded on the system, what was going on in that room. Of course, he could anytime watch the activities inside the room live, but he had never done so in the past. He would not do unless somebody had hinted that something was going on in the room. Then it was also really mysterious as to how the vendor engineer and the girl sneaked into the server room with Rajendran's key. Rajendran was also not there to throw any light and his phone was unreachable, as he was busy with his interview. But this was a really serious matter. It was a blunder, which would have otherwise attracted a major punishment, including sacking from the job. But, under the changed scenario, no action, let alone major punishment, seemed possible, as it would contradict their stand and the FIR filed subsequently.

In the afternoon, as expected, I was called by the DFO. I knew that I would be thoroughly grilled for various serious lapses. So I took the recording system AMC vendor report with me. As soon as he asked me to sit, I told him the whole story of what I had done since previous night with the recording system. 'Oh very intelligent of you,' he remarked about my ingenuity. When I told him that now it had been fixed and showed him the AMC vendor's recording system report. He also felt highly relieved. 'Good.' He then asked me about Rajendran, in a milder tone now than I imagined. I felt that by telling the story about recording system beforehand, I was definitely able to cut some ice, making the atmosphere lighter. I told him that he was on leave. 'How could they enter with

Rajendran's key?' he asked me.

'Yes sir, it is a real mystery. Let Rajendran come, he may be able to throw some light on it,' I said.

'But you also did not notice them either entering the server room or roaming there,' the DFO said bit tersely.

'Yes sir. In fact, I was not there for some time, and had just arrived before you. I had gone to Bajpai's department,' I told him.

'Something official?'

'Yes, I had gone there to discuss something, then had a cup of tea with him, so it took some time,' I clarified.

'You see, these people are pestering me to take stringent action against Rajendran for allowing unauthorized persons inside the server room with his key and calling for your explanation in dereliction of your duties. Of course, I have told them that it is not possible to give it in writing, as it would totally contradict our stand with the police and the media, unnecessarily dragging the FTMO's name. But our serious concern is if something had happened otherwise, it being so critical to our operations. If they had fiddled with any of our system or data, then we would have been doomed,' he said, and further added after a pause, 'Though now there is no evidence of anyone being inside the server room, but Rajendran's key's entry is still there on the records.'

'So what, Rajendran himself entered the server room in the course of his normal duties,' I suggested my line of defence.

'Was he there yesterday?'

'Yes sir, he was very much there. He had left in the afternoon. In fact, everything had happened in a short span of time, when he had just left, and I was not there,' I told him.

'But it is very serious...'

'Yes sir, no doubt about it,' I repentantly said. Though I very much wanted to know how he got inkling to the activities inside the server room, I had no guts to ask him. I was still in this dilemma, when his PA informed him that there was a call from the central office, Mumbai, and I left his room.

While coming back from his office, his words 'had they fiddled with our system' were continuously resonating in my ears and so I directly dashed to the server room. I started checking various terminals, one by one, and I got a shock of my life when I opened the recording of the webcam of the monitoring terminal. The girl could be hazily seen sitting on the terminal. Of course, it was for a very short while, and nothing more could be made out from the recording despite my playing it repeatedly. I was in a fix, about what I should do—share this information with the DFO or simply erase it without taking note of it or replace the terminal. I did not unnecessarily want to share it when nothing discerning could be made out from it. On the other hand, I did not want to erase it in a hurry. Replacing the terminal immediately was also not possible as it was a Saturday and Rajendran was not there. But, at the same time, I did not want to leave it, as anybody could see it if he wanted to. So I decided to do what we did once earlier also—render the display non-functional, postponing the final action for Monday when Rajendran would also be there. I replaced the display fuse with a blown-off one; so that nobody could see the recording, at least till Monday.

Meanwhile, I again received a call on my intercom from the DFO secretariat saying that the DFO wanted to see me. On reaching there, he told me, 'I have called you to share another development. I received a phone call from the central office after you left. Somebody has passed on to them the actual sequence of yesterday's events, aggravating our problems further.'

I very abruptly and stupidly asked, 'Then sir?'

'No, I told them that some of us had definitely seen her running towards the staircase, but to avoid the FTMO's name being unnecessarily dragged into it, it was not mentioned to the police. Moreover, it was not relevant to the case,' the DFO told me.

'Sir.'

'There is no trace left of them in the server room?' asked the DFO a little restlessly. This was one question, which put me totally out of my mind. It was very difficult to decide and reply to this in 'yes' or 'no'. The DFO was looking desperately at me, waiting for my confirmation.

'Yes-yes, no-no sir,' I said in haste, totally confused.

'What do you mean?' the DFO said little irritated.

'I mean sir, yes, no trace is left.'

'Sure?'

'Yes sir,' I said very firmly as by now I had decided to stick to my earlier decision of postponing the matter till Monday. He looked greatly relieved. Feeling that the atmosphere was now little congenial, I wanted to ask how he had got the inkling to the activities inside the server room but I still could not find enough courage. Gathering all my courage, when I was just about to ask him this, there was again a call from the central office, and I left his room once again.

24

The Longest Day

Sunday was the longest day of my life. I did not know what to do. Bajpai and Das were not there to share my anxieties. Bajpai had just gone on LFC; Das had already been away to his native place for his son's admission. Rajendran had not returned after his interview. I did not know what view the central office would lay about the episode. Would they come to know what had happened in the server room? Would they be able to find and establish any link between the two events—happenings inside the server room and the suicide? If so, what action would be taken against us? Who were the people behind it? Who had instigated the DFO to check the recording of the server room activities? We were clueless about the girl and her motive. How did she fall? Was it just an accident, or had she jumped herself, or had she been pushed? Would the police take it as a simple case of suicide in isolation and close the case or probe deeper into it? And if the police linked it to the happenings of the server room what would be our fate? Would we land behind bars? More so, what if they did come to know about our earlier server room misadventures when we had tried to link it from terminal outside. All these questions were agitating my mind and I was restless. I was feeling like a convict waiting for the judgement to be pronounced; and had the limited options of being hanged or to be shot.

When you are agitated and hurt, you start analyzing yourself, your traits, your surroundings, your roots, and past events, in an attempt to relate your present woes to the past. And this was exactly what was happening inside me then. I remembered Das had commented once—'you have now earned more foes than ever. People are already after you for taking so many pangas as you have provoked them a number of times.' Perhaps, he was right. Somehow, I had the habit of throwing stones in a still pond to see its reactions. Where was the need to apply filters so rigorously and block all the sites, thus denying people from making their few extra bucks from the share market? After all, money did not grow on trees ...though in my childhood I was convinced that it did grow on plants. Why did I bluntly refuse to oblige the staff by loaning three to four PCs for a day or two for their union meet? Why did I take it as a personal challenge to maintain the continuity of all the computers operations during the one-day strike, totally sabotaging their efforts and ensuring that their strike is a complete flop? Then, the sincere advice given by Bajpai—'You should do your job alright, but avoid hurting the sentiments of others openly and blatantly. Do things quietly as far as possible, without involving yourself in direct confrontation with the people.' But was it possible for me to do so? Perhaps not. I was as blunt as ever and took things head on, never caring who was being antagonized in the process. Though a second-generation city migrant, I had yet to acquire that finesse, that sophistication, howsoever pseudo, which was must for smooth-sailing in any metropolitan environment. More often than not, I was tagged for my totally unpolished, non-diplomatic, rude but straight behaviour that was anyway of no consequence. As they said, I was not at all worldly-wise, and was so straight and blunt that I could go to any extent, even harming my own interests. Otherwise, I would have not risked linking the server room terminal with the terminal outside, simply out of a childlike inquisitiveness. Perhaps, that was why I was often called 'Kalidas'.

'Why am I not smooth sailing? Why is my life always full of choppiness? Why is it always me? Why am I inquisitive to the limit of stupidity? Am I facing such an unnerving situation for the first time? Is it in isolation, or a sequel to a chain of past events? Has it been there since my childhood? Yes, I have been inquisitive since childhood', I remembered, when I tried to grow money on trees. These thoughts were unnerving me. When you feel insecure, so unnerved, you tend to dig into your roots, your family, past, and your childhood, to seek answers and solace there so that you may put the blame squarely on your past for all your present woes. I was lost in my early memories...

'From childhood till date, my life has been full of dilemmas, conflicts, and contradictions. It has been a long story of anxieties and struggles, at times internal and sometimes external. I remember how I used to suffer from complexes due to these repressed feelings in my childhood and how I overcame them over a period of time with maturity. My childhood was full of incidents, some as hilarious as how once my mother declared me hard of hearing to save a situation; or as curious as trying to grow money on plants. This childhood incident of growing money has been engraved in my memory forever, as I still wonder why money cannot grow on trees!

As a child, I was as inquisitive as I am today. I had one great illusion that it was possible to cultivate money. For this, I would dig a hole in the front lawns of my house, and then bury the old one-paisa coin, one with a hole in the centre, expecting that trees full of coins would grow. This one-paisa coin was in use at that time and remained in circulation until early sixties. Next day, I would inspect the earth for the coins and would be satisfied when I did not find them there. I thought that the coins would have dissolved into the earth ready for stems to grow out. I kept waiting for plants to grow, but it never happened. And to my great surprise, I would not find a single coin there next day.

Meanwhile, my mother noticed that she was not finding the one-paisa coins with the holes, among other coins. She found out that it was I who was removing them. When she asked me, I told her everything about my experiment including the name of my mentor, a Pahari family servant (incidentally, his name was Maniram), under whose directions the project was being conducted. It took her no time to unfold the mystery and the whole project came to a sudden halt. I still feel that had my guru not removed the coins from the earth and had he left them to germinate, the experiment would have been a success. Alas! The experiment cannot be tried now, as there are no more holed coins, perfectly fit for germination. Though I failed in my venture, I still believe that money does grow.

....Then there the feelings mere of insecurity creeping in because of my father's the frequent transfers and the family being away, stationed at one place to complete the children's education...then trying to understand those unusual sounds, muffled cries and creaking of the charpoy in the night... and then the wet dreams in the mid of my sleep...and bunking school on some pretext or other just to enjoy the onslaught of puberty full time...

...and then hearing 'Grandma-tips' from my hiding place under the quilt on the bed, while elderly women discussed lewd and obscene things, though I was unable to understand much then.

'I have told my niece that the best cure for avoiding pimples...is to press and rub 'that' between two fingers there to release the body heat...'

'From her face and behaviour I could immediately make out that she was not fully satisfied with her man...and suggested her to try the "woman on top" position...'

'I have suggested her to just quietly slip "his" inside "hers" early morning when "it" is hard on its own and he is fast asleep, if he is avoiding to have a child right now...'

...and so on

Slowly, my personality developed into that of an introvert—an insecure and an unsocial person who suffered from complexes because of being excessively protected by my family during my formative years, and no one being there to share my repressed feelings.

Born in a large joint family, I was brought-up in a highly protected environment. Being the youngest amongst my siblings, I was the darling of the whole family. The treatment bestowed on me was so special and exclusive that over a period, in a way, it isolated me from the other members of the family and made me think that I was different from the lot, instilling a feeling of superiority in me. When in formative years you are protected so much and treated so exclusively, you tend to develop a shell around yourself, which insulates you from the harsh realities of life. But by hiding yourself, the world doesn't cease to exist. Therefore, in the later years of life, when this shell is subjected to the usual pulls and pressures of reality, you suddenly find questioning yourself and feeling insecure developing all sorts of complexes. So much so, I started feeling rivalry and insecure towards anybody and everybody, including my kin, childhood friends, and my classmates. Perhaps, that resulted in striving harder to maintain my number one position anyhow, to total absurdity, just to maintain my image as projected by my close family members. Luckily, all along I had very understanding and supportive people around me. (Parents, especially mothers, I feel, should desist from the tendency to project their wards which may put them under unnecessary pressure to perform and prove true to this image.)

This crisis of existence, of an 'identity' was not only raging within me but was also there in my roots. I am not the first one in my family to face such a crisis, nor was my family's past very straight or upright. The only thing is that, people are not aware of it.

How our forefathers acquired our surname is another story. Murdering all seven members of a family and then accepting religion in penance!

As the story goes, a religion that propounded non-violence was adopted only some seven generations back by one of our great grandfathers as a matter of repentance after murdering all the seven members of a family, when he was caught having an intimate relationship with a woman of that family. Before surrendering in the court to an English judge for confessing the crime, he accepted this religion in penance, swore by the newly- accepted vow of non-violence, and turned down any plea for leniency and mercy. He was hanged!

Of course, nobody at Kanpur knows about this past of ours and everyone takes us to be a family of white collared, well-cultured people, sometimes even mistaking us to the extent of being a family of highly educated and intellectual members. Nothing can be a far cry from that.

Neither did anyone know how my family had migrated from the village to the city to keep the child (my father) away from the shadow of evil spirit as the previous off springs had not survived. He was sent away from the village for his studies, never to return!

And hats off to my father—born in a village where there was no electricity, or road, he was the first to read and write, and who had the guts to land in Kanpur at the height of World War II, recognizing a great opportunity for life insurance business, and succeeding amazingly. He was a totally self-made man, who moved on with courage and conviction throughout his life, never compromising on his principles and values.'

A phone call broke the chain of my thoughts, though these past reflections had reassured and calmed me, reminding me that I had the same blood of 'never-say-die' running in my veins.

It was a call from an unknown number. I picked up it, 'Hullo, Mr Rajesh! I am Kaushik Mukherjee calling, a relative of your Kanpur neighbour Mr Banerjee. Do you remember me?'

'Yes-yes. How are you Mr Mukherjee?' I tried to place

him, recollecting his relationship with my neighbour.

'I am good... I wanted to meet you sir, regarding the suicide, but then did not think it would be proper to call you at office, as people would come to know about it immediately. For the same reason, I did not come to your house since you stay in the bank's colony. I wanted to warn you about these people's evil designs,' Mr Mukherjee made his intention clear. 'These people, now feeling a setback because of the police registering only a case of suicide in isolation, without connecting it to the server room happenings, were murmuring about doing something. They will try to re-open it. They can go to any extent to revive the case, so be careful sir.'

'But who prompted the DFO to open and watch the recorder out of the blue?' I asked him.

'I don't know exactly, but I presume it may be Mr Sikdar,' he expressed his suspicion.

'Mr Sikdar?' I was surprised at his guess.

'Yes. You must be very careful of Mr Sikdar. He is divided in his loyalty, in fact, he has no loyalty at all, as he only acts to promote his interests. He poses to be very close to the DFO, but at the same time, he has very strong connections with the union. He is a two-faced character, a very dangerous person indeed.'

'Oh, I see.'

'Yes, he is not to be trusted at all for anything,' he cautioned me.

'And what happened to the vendor engineer, any idea about his whereabouts?'

'He must be in their captivity I guess, or at least under their control.'

'Maybe...'

'You can call me on this number anytime, other than office hours.'

'Thank you so much Mr Mukherjee for calling,' and I hung up the phone.

25

Curtain Raiser I

Early on Monday morning, Rajendran called me from the train and told me that his train was running late and so he would be reaching office late. So I started preparing to reach office early. Anyway, I wanted to avoid meeting people on my way to office, or in the office lifts, or corridors and facing their piercing questions.

Police officials were busy inspecting the parking site, when I entered the office premises. I did not take note of it and headed towards the lift's lobby. In the lobby, I was told that the DFO had also arrived. After reaching my department, I checked all the systems, as usual. Everything was in the same position, including the monitoring terminal display, as I had left it on Saturday. As I was about to call Rajendran to know his position, my intercom rang. It was a call from the DFO secretariat saying that the DFO wanted to see me if I had arrived. On reaching he told me, 'I have called you to say that I had again received a phone call on Saturday evening from the central office, when you had just left. Now, they have decided to send a team tomorrow, on Tuesday, to examine the security lapses. Though they are saying that it is just to examine the security aspect, I feel they will check everything including the server room. So be ready,' and after a pause added, as if trying to remember something, 'And your recording system is functioning as desired. I mean it has no recording of that day.'

'Yes sir,' I emphatically confirmed.

'But I feel there is a contradiction in the entire story. You have taken the recording system AMC vendor's report on Saturday, stating that the system had been down for the last three days, but on Friday evening, the vendor himself checked to see the system working all right. How could he modify his report to that effect so easily, when he must have already submitted his positive report on Friday?' asked the DFO very seriously.

'On Friday evening...but he never checked it on Friday evening,' I was completely baffled by his version.

'Then who asked us on Friday evening to check the recording system monitor of my room, to see if it was working all right,' the DFO asked, a little puzzled.

'What?...Somebody asked you to check it?' my jaw dropped and eyes widened in total disbelief.

'Yes, of course. Only then, I opened my monitor and noticed those happenings inside the server room, and rushed to you,' the DFO clarified the sequence of events.

'How did he ask you? Did he come here?'

'No, as usual my PA came to me and told me that he has been asked by the AMC vendor to check it,' and then the DFO called his PA and asked him 'Who called you on Friday evening to check the recording system?'

'Sir, the AMC vendor of the recording system,' replied his PA.

'Did he come to you?' the DFO asked.

'No sir, he asked me over the intercom,' clarified his PA.

'Oh,' the DFO took a long breath and said to his PA, 'Thank you.' When his PA left, I said, 'The AMC vendor was absent on Friday. In fact, on Saturday morning when he visited us, he told me that for the last two days he was away from town.'

'So the question of him visiting on Friday, and giving in any report does not arise.'

'Yes sir,' I said spiritedly, as now the mystery of the DFO getting inkling to the happenings of the server room had unfolded.

'That means somebody else impersonated him over the intercom to my PA.'

'Sir.'

'I think it was a well-planned ploy by someone...and the girl was planted there,' murmured the DFO.

'Sir, perhaps, we will come to know more about it once Rajendran comes,' I added in a receding tone.

'Yes, where is Rajendran? Has he not come today?' the DFO asked suddenly in a very loud tone.

'Sir, he will reach any moment. His train was delayed,' I informed him. He did not say anything further about Rejendran.

'Well, you get ready for tomorrow. Make sure that no trace is left of Friday's episode. We can very well stick to our version without any problem,' said the DFO and added after a little pause, 'Please tell me immediately if you learn anything further in this regard.' He further warned me in a whispering tone, '... And mind you, keep it to yourself that we have already sensed some conspiracy, some mischief...'

After returning to my department, my first anxiety was

to do something about the monitoring terminal, but I waited for Rajendran before I decided to do anything about it. I was about to call him, when I saw him arrive. Before I could say anything, he himself said, 'I know.'

'Oh, I see...First, tell me how was your interview?' I snapped at him, thinking that he must have been told by the people about what had happened here, on his way to the department.

'Hopefully, soon you get rid of me sir...but I will definitely miss your good company.'

'Oh, good, tea or coffee?'

'Anything.'

I ordered for tea from the canteen over the intercom, 'Now tell me what do you know and who told you all that?' I asked him. And what he told me was yet another shocking revelation to me. In fact, someone had phoned him the previous evening itself, while he was still in the train, as his well-wisher. The caller had told him about the incident in short and then advised him as his well-wisher that he (Rajendran) should claim, that, he had passed on his key (password) to me before leaving on Friday. This way, all the blame would come on me and he could escape unscathed.

'Oh, I see,' I said and narrated to him the verbatim description of the events, since Friday. I also told him what the DFO told me this morning and how someone acting as the AMC vendor, had tricked them into opening the recording system.

'Sir, where is the recording stick, which you had replaced? I want to replay it to see the details of my entry and that girl,' asked Rajendran.

'That recording stick must be with the DFO, as I had removed and handed it to him on Friday night itself. We will ask him when we meet him later today. Meanwhile, you can do one thing; you can see her on the monitoring terminal webcam, though the picture is a bit hazy. Thank God, I have not deleted it,' I said, and added, 'And mind you to replace the fuse of its display first, as I told you that I had removed it and replaced it with a blown one.'

After seeing it, he said, 'It seems that only recently I had seen her waiting outside the FTMO. Perhaps, she must be the same girl, whom we saw strolling with him around Park Street, the previous night during the last strike'

'It is not much of consequence now. The important thing right now is what we can do with the monitoring terminal,' I said.

'I think let us keep the webcam recording, as it is for the time being, and change the terminal itself. Anyway, the original monitoring terminal has been fixed and is ready for use,' said Rajendran.

'Okay, we will replace it in the evening,' I said.

'Right sir...But how could they enter with my key? It's really intriguing,' said Rajendran.

'Yes. Perhaps, he had stolen it,' I said.

'It so then they must have entered after I had left,' he said.

'Yes, of course,' I endorsed him.

'It can be confirmed from the details of entry, but we don't have the recording stick with us now,' he expressed his helplessness and then suddenly, realizing something he spiritedly added, 'But this can be seen even from the log details of the door lock. Yes, let us take the log printout of the door lock.'

When we checked the details, there was no entry of Rajendran's key, after he had left. It clearly confirmed that they had not entered it.

'That means your key was not stolen,' I said.

'Yes'

'Then what? Did they enter with you?' I said a little baffled.

'Yes one thing. The vendor engineer was well aware of my programme, and entered with me, and was there with me until I left. However, there was no girl. Moreover, he also left with me,' said Rajendran, remembering the sequence of events that day.

'But do you clearly remember that he also left with you,' I asked.

'Certainly. I have never left him alone there. There is no chance,' Rajendran said very emphatically, and then immediately added, 'Let us check the door movement details also.'

As soon as we started checking the door movement details, Rajendran jumped out of his chair, 'Here it is! See the door was opened at 3.50 and remained open until 5.55. The bugger must have inserted something between the door and its frame, while leaving with me at 3.50 to block the door from being latched completely. When I left and after some time you went, he must have sneaked in with the girl sometime between 3.50 and 5.55 in our absence. As the door was not locked, so no key was required to enter this time,' Rajendran solved the mystery of their entry completely.

'Let us go and tell the DFO about it,' I said excitedly.

'Do I also need to come?' asked Rajendran.

I thought for a while and then said, 'You do one thing;

you come with me and wait there at the DFO secretariat. When he asks about you, then I will call you.'

'That's better,' agreed Rajendran.

I called the DFO's PA to know if anyone else was there with him and if we could go there.

When he said, 'Right now, there is no one,' we went there with the door lock log printout.

As soon as I entered his chamber, he eagerly asked, 'Yes Rajesh, any development?'

'Yes sir, Rajendran is here and we have solved the mystery of the entry into the server room,' I said spiritedly.

'Oh that's very good. Where is Rajendran?' he said excitedly.

'He is here too.'

'Then call him. Why is he outside?'

I immediately called Rajendran inside and explained to the DFO in complete detail what must have happened on Friday. Then I also told him about the phone call that Rajendran had received on Sunday evening, while he was still in the train.

'Oh it is no less than a conspiracy, I say and that too very well planned and hatched,' said the DFO.

'Sir,' I agreed and added, 'Sir, can we have the recording stick for some time, as we want to see something?'

'Recording stick?...Which recording stick?' the DFO said bewildered.

'Sir the same stick related to the episode, which I replaced and handed to you on Friday evening, after you asked me to replace it,' I tried to remind him about the sequence of events.

'But...but did you give it to me? Of course, I asked you to replace it,' he said trying to recollect.

'Yes sir, when Mr Sikdar, who dealt with the police, was also here. In fact, he insisted that you must keep it, when you tried to return it to me,' I repeated the sequence of events.

'Yes...yes...perhaps...but where is it?' and then the DFO started searching his table, its drawers and then the side cabinets, but it was not there. He then called his PA, 'Did I give you something, some memory stick type thing to keep, on that evening, Friday evening?'

'Friday evening...No sir, not to me,' replied the PA.

'Call the Liaison Officer,' the DFO instructed his PA. He repeated the same question to him, but when he replied in the negative, he, the DFO called his PS on the intercom asking him the same question. He also expressed his total ignorance about it. When I saw the DFO was getting quite agitated about it, I said, 'Leave it sir, it is not required.'

'But we must get it,' the DFO expressed concern.

'Sir... but we will search for it, after the central office team leaves tomorrow,' I said.

'Okay...but I will check it here again, in the evening,' the DFO said and we left.

After reaching our department, Rajendran commented, 'How was it misplaced. I wonder...'

'It is possible. There was complete confusion on that day and everyone was unnerved...,' I said.

'I hope it is not again a part of the game. We must take all precautions,' Rajendran expressed his apprehensions.

'Yes, we must, as it has all the evidence of...' I agreed.

We replaced the monitoring terminal in the evening and checked that everything was in desired order for the central office inspection the next day. Meanwhile, there was another development. In the evening, I received a call from our New York office stating that their system had detected some duplicate entries (of forex deals credit) in the string (of forex transactions) of Friday, which they had deleted though. However, to be doubly sure, they advised me to check it manually at our end as well, for any other duplicate entries left to be deleted. They were advising me on Monday about the Friday transactions string, Saturday being off for forex deals. I was again in a dilemma whether to share this information with the DFO or not. First, I thought that we would quietly check it ourselves, but realizing that task was enormous and could not be completed, without pooling help from the others, I decided to take the DFO into confidence, but in my own way. I told the DFO that to be doubly sure, before the central office inspection I wanted to check the Friday string manually, for any discrepancy of duplicate entries etc., as an abundant precaution for which I required help. He immediately mobilized people from other departments to put on the task. However, I did not say anything about the detection of duplicate entries at our New York office, but still there were some who smelled something amiss and were curious to know the real reason for this exercise.

Mr Sikdar immediately commented, 'Why, what happened? Did you detect something?'

When I tried to repeat the same plea of precautionary check he at once retorted, 'Such a mammoth exercise just for a precautionary check? It is not possible. The central office people are not going to do all this! Who has time for all this? Unless you have actually detected something, this is a total waste of our resources and has no point.' When he threatened to leave, I had to tell him the actual reason and he was satisfied. It took us well beyond midnight to complete checking of all the Friday transactions, but thank God, we did not find any other duplicate entry.

The next day when the central office team examined the security lapses, they also demanded to inspect the server room, as expected. They replayed the recorder and when they asked why there was no recording for the last three days, they were told that it was down, and was fixed on Saturday.

'But why did it take so long to get it fixed? Why was the complaint not lodged immediately with the AMC vendor?' they probed.

'The complaint was lodged immediately, but the engineer was out of town for two days. That is why it took three days to get it fixed,' and they were shown the AMC vendor's report.

They did not think it necessary to probe further and we, including the DFO, heaved a sigh of relief. Then they also checked the recording of webcams on various terminals and did not find anything incriminating. Fortunately, it did not occur to them to check the log printout of the door. However, it would have not thrown any light on the activities of the room, but still it could have clearly shown them that the door had been open for so long. And it was definitely a security lapse for which we had no sustainable answer. Thus, the inspection went off well, without any hitch. Though they did comment on the security lapses of the security agency, which had allowed the girl to sneak in and reach the nineteenth floor, but then it was the remark on the functions of the external security agency, which anyway had been changed immediately.

26

Curtain Raiser II

The central office inspection proved to be a great blow to all those, who were behind the conspiracy or against us and wanted our heads. We were given a clean chit in their report, when it was received after five-six days. In a way, they complimented us, the Computers Group, for introducing various filters. In fact, emboldened by the report, the DFO even refused to acknowledge the incident before some office people, who asked to him about the status of action against us.

'What action, what for? A girl sneaked in and committed suicide. How are they responsible for this? The security agency was responsible for the lapses, and its service has been terminated,' he told them.

'But how about that girl being found in the server room?' they asked.

'I have no idea, as nothing is mentioned in the report to that effect,' the DFO expressed his ignorance.

So far so good. But the crucial recording stick could not be traced still, despite it being rigorously searched. The police ultimately traced the antecedents of that girl to a mini red-light area. Meanwhile, Rajendran received his selection intimation for the new job. Things had almost quietened and settled down, and more than a fortnight had passed since the incident.

We were now busy on two projects. One, to finalize the deal for the alternate system on hire, to replace the existing main servers until the new ones were bought in. Two, to drop and finalize the proposal for the contingency mirror site (an alternate standby site, replicating the primary site and to be used in case of emergency) as part of the contingency plan. As it was taking time to finalize the location, for the permanent full scale contingency site at Belapur, Mumbai, Thane or Chennai, it was decided to have a transit, local site for the FTMO at the Salt Lake Regional Office immediately. Rajendran was told that he would be relieved for his new job, only when the basic spadework for these two projects was completed. We were in the thick of working on these projects, almost having forgotten about the server room incident, when one afternoon, I received a call from the DFO secretariat that a team of police officials had landed in connection with the suicide. They were sitting with the DFO, who immediately asked for me. I was told that police officials wanted to see the recording system and play the recordings of that period. I told them that they could come with me to the server room. Meanwhile, I informed Rajendran over the phone that we were all coming to the department to see the recordings.

After checking the recording system, they asked us to replay the recordings of that period. On replaying, they found that there was no recording for those three days; and asked us why. They were told that the system had been down and could be fixed only on the next day after the incident, and were shown the AMC vendor's report to that effect.

'But we have been told by an anonymous letter that the recording that you have here is not the original one.

The informer has also sent a recording stick to us, claiming it to be the original one. We would like to run this on the recording system,' one of the police officials said, and took the stick out from his briefcase. As soon as he took it out, we unmistakably recognized it. We were stunned. I was completely dumbfounded. I never expected this even in my wildest dreams. I could clearly see the sweat on the DFO's reddened face. When he again asked to replay that recording stick, Rajendran calmly came forward and took the stick from him, as I continued to stand like a dumb statue with widened eyes, no expressions, whatsoever, on my face. Rajendran replaced the stick and pushed the 'play' button on the recorder. We waited breathlessly for it to run, but there were no signs of recordings. And after some time, it displayed 'No data'. The police official himself tried to replay it, but 'No data' was repeatedly displayed. They tried to replay it thrice, but to no avail. We could not believe our eyes. It was like a miracle for us. The police officials sat down, now completely exhausted and cheated by the misinformation. Before taking out and returning the stick to the police officials, Rajendran again tried once or twice to run it. The police officials took the stick back. They apologized for the unnecessary trouble and left. I was so excited that I could just stop myself from saying that it was our missing stick, when the police official asked for the stick back. The news of the recording stick turning out to be blank spread like a wild fire in the FTMO.

Late in the afternoon, both of us were called by the DFO. He straight away asked why the stick did not run. I gestured to Rajendran to reply what he had already told me, just then in the department. 'Sir, in fact, when we could not trace the stick that day, I immediately smelt a rat and decided to do something. The next day, after the central office team left, I changed the profile settings of the recording system, turning all the available sticks with us compatible with the new settings. Of course, this stick was not there and hence it was incompatible with the settings. And if a stick is incompatible with the settings of the recording system, it will never run on that system, and would display a blank screen,' explained Rajendran.

'Superb! Now the only thing left is that it still has a recording, but that doesn't matter as it won't run anywhere,' said the DFO excitedly.

'But even that data has now been quietly erased, when he ran the stick again after police officials had tried,' I added enthusiastically.

'Rajendran when do you want to be relieved?' asked the DFO feeling very happy with his smartness and for saving all of us unimaginable consequences.

'Sir, as early as possible,' replied Rajendran.

'Then what would happen to the contingency site project?' the DFO teased him and Rajendran just grinned cheek to cheek.

'Okay let the police closure report arrive and I will relieve you. I hope to get it in four to five days,' assured the DFO. 'But I wonder how the stick reached their hands,' he said further, after a pause.

'I think somebody removed it from here and then passed it on to them... maybe, I cannot say for sure Mr Sikdar who negotiated with the police... I have been told now that he has very close relations with some of the union people as well,' I said, in a receding tone.

'Just possible...anything is possible,' agreed the DFO.

'In fact, if you remember sir, he insisted that you must keep it, when you tried to return it to me,' I repeated the sequence of events.

'Yes-yes,' endorsed the DFO and added, 'This only completes half the story. The vendor engineer is still missing and absconding from his company. What exactly happened with the girl is still not known.'

After a few days, a copy of the police closure report was received and we were called by the DFO. He told us about the report and then enquired about the status of the contingency site. 'Sir, hopefully, the transit local site at the Salt Lake regional office should be ready for partial operations in a few weeks. But for full operations, it would take a few months. As far as the final site is concerned, the central office is yet to decide about the location, whether Belapur Mumbai, Thane or Chennai,' I apprised him with the position.

'Okay forget about the final site, until it is decided by the central office, but complete the Salt Lake one as fast as possible. You never know when it may be required. What is the position?' asked the DFO.

'Sir, except for the servers, which were to come from Mumbai, as per plan, everything is in the pipeline and progressing as per schedule,' I informed.

'If the servers are not received from Mumbai in time, which anyway I don't expect, then?' the DFO said a bit anxiously.

'Then in that case as a stopgap arrangement, we may divert the rented servers hired for replacing our existing servers at the FTMO to Salt Lake contingency site and very well utilize until we get these from Mumbai, as rented servers are of similar configuration and capacity,' I suggested.

'Oh that is great. Go ahead,' said the DFO greatly relieved, and then added, 'And how about the contingency plan for the Computers Group, I mean a substitute for Rajendran, as he is to be relieved now.'

Then turning towards Rajendran, the DFO asked, 'This weekend will do?' And Rajendran nodded his head.

As assured, Rajendran was relieved for his new job.

The missing vendor engineer continued to abscond from his company. Later, his mutilated body was found in a pond at the outskirts of the city.

27

Missing Link

'Where were you buggers, I say?' I said excitedly, on meeting Bajpai and Das after a long time.

'It seems a lot of water has flown in the Hooghly in our absence,' Das said.

'Let us go to my desk and have tea,' Bajpai offered.

They wanted to know all the details of the incident sequentially, when we reached there.

'Though we have come to know about the whole episode, but in pieces,' said Bajpai.

'Moreover, we want to hear from the horse's mouth itself,' Das seconded Bajpai.

I narrated the entire story and ended it with telling them that they were again planning to go on strike.

'Oh that is old news. Latest is that they are divided over it, as there are two groups, one is moderate, but the other one is quite aggressive,' Bajpai said.

'But I will tell you something more confidential,' said Das, gesturing us to come close, and adding in a guarded, whispering tone, 'That moderate group is quite disappointed over the way they hatched the conspiracy, taking that girl's life first and then the vendor engineer's...'

Meanwhile, our tea had arrived. 'But what exactly

happened to that girl, how did she fall?' I was curious to know their version.

'Perhaps, it was an accident, as she hit the staircase balcony railing in the rush and tumbled over it,' said Bajpai and then added almost murmuring, 'But as per the other version, the vendor engineer bumped her off wanting to keep the entire money with him.'

'But I think to make the incident widely public, this was also part of the plan and the vendor engineer acted accordingly, as was also hinted in the murmurings of the other group,' added Das quietly.

'Oh,' I said sadly and added bit hesitantly in a whispering tone, 'But I have something more to share... to complete the story. This is my inference and conjecture based on my observations that there was something more to it, and it was not simply to malign me, but it had a deeper design and wider ramifications. What we saw on the surface was just the eyewash.'

'Really! Please...' they said in unison.

'I have not shared this with anyone. This, for the first time, I am sharing with anyone and expect you people to keep it strictly with you only. I told you that while checking the Server Room, after the incident, for tampering with the systems, I found in the webcam recording a girl sitting there. And I told you that later, I received a message from our New York office that they had detected few duplicate entries in that day's string. This immediately got me suspicious as to if they had some deeper sinister designs, as it at once reminded me of our earlier Server Room misadventure, when we had tried to watch a porno graphic site from outside the room. I had also linked the Server Room monitoring terminal to my terminal outside for mirroring and controlling. Perhaps, they were also trying to do somewhat the same thing, to control the monitoring terminal from one outside, so that they could send fake entries from that terminal in future, as part of high-level conspiracy, for transferring large sums fraudulently. Only thing is that our software was a do-it-yourself feel-version kit, of limited capability, and theirs must have been fully functional and professional. And on trial basis, they succeeded also by sending duplicate entries from the terminal outside. But fortunately for us, they did not live to carry out their plan of actually sending fake entries later. I immediately smelt something deeper, when I saw the webcam recordings and everything became very evident, once I came to know about duplicate entries. In fact, now I also recollected seeing the computer warning "Installation file of similar software already exists" when I was loading my kit. But then I did not take notice of it as I was totally engrossed in installing of my own software to link the server room monitoring terminal to terminal outside. Moreover, I could never have thought of this even in my dreams. I realized it only once this incident took place. Putting all the pieces together, I immediately visualized their entire plan and unfolded the high-level conspiracy for a computerized scam, due to our experience of the earlier misadventure. In fact, the misadventure really proved to be a boon in disguise, as I could at once sniff of something wrong. But all this, I could not share with anyone and claim its possibility as nobody was aware of our earlier misadventure. More so, as it would have had very serious repercussions on us, for grave dereliction of our duties in maintaining the room's security and sanctity, if I had disclosed and elaborated this conspiracy, having been solely responsible.'

'That means some other force was also functional,' said Das.

'Definitely, I presume. In fact, the engineer apparently was working for the union as a cover, but actually, he was working for someone else for larger purposes. And in all possibility, the union people did not have inkling about the engineer's sinister designs. Their main purpose was to malign the Computers Group by showing a breach of the most secured and totally restricted area of the main server room by some outsider.'

'You mean to say that the breach of the room and the death of the girl were two separate events and unrelated,' asked Das.

'Not exactly, but to a certain extent, yes. The breach was common to both the plots, but later events were circumstantial to the union's plot.'

'But then if the girl's death and subsequent arrival of the police on the scene were not part of the original union plot, and not thought of earlier, then how did the recording stick reach the police so swiftly?' probed Das.

'Perhaps, not thought of as systematically as it happened, and most likely, it was the ingenuity of Mr Sikdar. Later, when in the wake of sudden developments, he saw a chance to settle his personal score as well with the Computers Group. He immediately swung into action and thought of swindling away the recording stick and made sure it reached the police, in connivance with the union people.'

'And the girl?'

'The girl was hired by the engineer just to misguide all of us. The girl was brought by him mainly to sit on the terminal and operate it. The girl was bumped off, perhaps by the engineer himself, because she learned about his actual sinister designs and could be dangerous for him, or would have demanded a higher cut. Only thing, their plan misfired, perhaps because of some other enthusiastic union activist, who in excitement informed the DFO a little before the schedule. I feel as per the plan, the DFO was to be informed about the server room happenings, only when they would have left. And perhaps then, the union people would have confidently told the DFO about this as a breach by Rajendran's girlfriend, blaming Rajendran squarely, and in turn the Computers Group directly. Anyway, the room was accessed through Rajendran's key and that was why the DFO had immediately asked for Rajendran and suspected him to be there with a girl. Moreover, earlier also, Rajendran was found with his girlfriend in the computers' dump room and the DFO was aware of this incident. Thus, this incident would have carried a lot of weight. And you never know, this mess might be deliberate, to dilute the case—a result of inter-union rivalry of two groups, to showdown each other, as you mentioned.'

'But you did not notice anything abnormal or unusual while checking the systems, after the incident, though you came to know about the webcam recordings,' asked Bajpai.

'Well… I may admit that while checking for any tampering of the monitoring terminal, I did find traces of fiddling and links with it, though it was not actually linked then. He must have de-linked it, after linking, and sending a few duplicate entries as test ones, so that it would not be noticed. All this—installing of mirroring software, linking, sending of duplicate entries, then de-linking, and uninstalling of the software, must have been done between 3.50 to 5.55 p.m., when the door of the server room was open, as per the log. The engineer was aware of Rajendran's programme and the entire thing was timed, according to when Rajendran would have left. Their game plan must have been to first try sending some duplicate entries as test entries, from outside the room, by linking the monitoring terminal, and if it succeeded, then they would have actually sent fictitious entries later. And for this, they wanted to confirm that their trial is being successful, before sending fictitious entries. This they would have learned from our department, only when our New York office, on the next working day would have alerted us about the detection of duplicate entries in the string, as it actually happened. So the terminal was de-linked in the intervening period and the status-quo was restored by undoing whatever was done for linking, including uninstalling of software, if any. Since the engineer was aware of the webcam recording on the monitoring terminal that was why he brought the girl with him and made her sit on the monitoring terminal. They would have carried out the actual plan of siphoning off funds through fictitious entries, sometime later, after the confirmation of their modus operandi being successful. While these duplicate entries could be detected by the system, at our New York office, but the actual fictitious ones, being unique, would have gone completely unnoticed. But the entire plan fizzled out, due to the over enthusiasm of some union member, or maybe inter-union rivalry, and that opportunity did not arise.'

'Oh... But the engineer was also eliminated,' said Bajpai.

'Naturally. When the entire plan failed, and there was no chance left to carryout this scam, the engineer became a great risk, aware of everything. How he could have been spared! Before he could spill the beans, he was also eliminated.'

'It is a startling revelation that the plot was actually laid as a cover up for a high level computerized scam and a well thought of plan. So that completes the story, with a wonderful inference, and a conclusion.' Both heaved a long sigh of relief.

'Yes, but it will always remain a mystery as to who were the people as the third force behind the engineer's misdeeds.'

28

Cherian Responds

Though every bit had fallen into place completing the picture of the attempted scam plan, I still wanted to confirm my observations about the possibility of actually sending fictitious entries later, as per the foiled scam plan, when I received an email from Cherian in response to my earlier email:

Dear Rajesh,

Happy to know that you could try the 'do-it-yourself' kit of the linking software. Hope you have enjoyed working with it, though it is of limited capability. In fact, I could not respond to your email earlier, as we were quite busy working with it to improvise it further. It has now grown many more times in its capability and functioning.

Please do let me know if you need anything from me and take care,

Cherian.

I immediately emailed back,

Dear Cherian,

Thank you for the mail. Can we chat tonight for a

while at 12.30 p.m., IST (your late afternoon time) to discuss an important issue related to such linking software.

Rajesh.

Cherian responded,
Done, Rajesh. Make it 11.30 p.m., IST.
Till then,
Cherian.
And we carried on our chat at night on the internet—

Me—Hi Cherian, I won't take much of your time. I just wanted to know whether it is possible for such linking software to duplicate any particular entry.

Cherian—Yes, with the advanced versions of this software, it is possible, as these are replicating and controlling software. But one should have little knowledge about the main loaded financial software also.

This may not be that easy with the 'do-it-yourself' kit, which I had sent you, as it was of very limited capability.

Me—Right...Now my main query—is it possible to send a fictitious entry also?

Cherian—Yes, with the more advanced versions of this software, it is possible to transmit a fake entry as well, if one is quite abreast with the functioning of the main software and has some idea about the code.

Naturally, this is unthinkable with the 'do-it-yourself' kit.

Me—Good. Thank you so much. Take care. Bye-bye.

Cherian—My pleasure. Bye.

29

Own Master

Meanwhile, one evening, unexpectedly, I received a phone call from my ex-colleague Pradeep, who had resigned from the FBI to start his own venture. He had had a lifetime's dream to do something of his own. He was manufacturing and exporting leather accessories to European countries. In fact, he had left the FBI at the time, when I was contemplating the same, after my unceremonious removal from Gorakhpur. I, of course, had ultimately decided to stay on for the time being.

'What boss, you are still hanging on to FBI, I am surprised,' Pradeep said, after an exchange of usual greetings.

'As of now, yes, I am pretty well settled in Cal, but let us see,' I said.

'Oh yes, I had heard about you being posted at FTMO, Cal. Recently, I came to know that you handled the situation very well during the one day strike there. Of course, it was expected of you, so I wasn't surprised at all, but that reminded me to call you. In fact, I was thinking about you for a long time, but somehow I could not call you. Now, this news excited me so much that I could not wait to call you.' Pradeep revealed how he remembered me.

'So nice of you to remember me. How are the things at your end?' I asked him.

'Doing well. Recently, I returned from Germany after visiting the Frankfurt Trade Fair. I am enjoying my work immensely. Here you have freedom; you decide your own direction. Since it is your own baby, so you work passionately to achieve your goals and then enjoy the results. Then you have to strive hard and be on your toes all the time. You are your own competitor. How about you? I know you are well settled and enjoying your Cal job, but then you too wanted to do something of your own. I feel that you have so much exposure in varied fields and so many skills, which can be better utilized otherwise.'

'You may be partly right, and I am also thinking on those lines, but for a middle-class person like me it is very difficult to leave the secured environment immediately. Is it not too risky?' I told him my problem.

'See boss, to achieve something you have to take a certain amount of risk. Either, take risk and grow, or be secured and stagnate. One shouldn't be scared to take risks, but learn to manage them. Then you have to weigh various available options. And in your case where is the risk? Your wife is well-settled in her teaching job; your son is almost about to complete his degree; you have no other liabilities, so where is the risk? Moreover, your service has become eligible for pension anyway, for whatever it is worth. See, I resigned my job without becoming pension-able.' Pradeep tried to motivate me by expounding on my doubts.

'Let me think where to begin.'

'As I remember, you had a passion for writing, and your short-stories and articles were published and well received also. Why don't you try something full length, sharing your experiences and feelings of your life?' Pradeep suggested.

I was really surprised that he also thought on similar lines as I did.

'Good idea. Let us see and wait for the right moment for some more time... I hope that I will be through my current project of the contingency site, as well as the impending strike soon. And then I may join your league.'

'Wish you all the best...bye'

'Thank you for calling and motivating me so much...bye, and take care.'

I felt that I was really approaching the opportune time to realize my lifetime's dream.

30

Next Round

After Rajendran's departure, I not only felt a void at a personal level, but was also found it difficult to maintain and manage the system on a day-to-day basis. I was yet to find a substitute for Rajendran, who could be given some responsibility, at least for day-to-day operations. Moreover, I was much more cautious now than ever and was taking abundant precautions, as far as the server room was concerned. Otherwise, I was also more vigilant in keeping track of all activities related to the Computers Group. I was scanning every report generated by the computers.

The new engineer provided by the vendor company, as a replacement of the earlier one was almost fresh, and not that experienced or fast as the earlier one. He was still in the process of not only learning about the job, but also familiarizing with the locations of various systems spread over fourteen floors. This further aggravated my problems. Of course, the server room was totally out of his bound. Because of all this, implementation work of the local contingency site was suffered badly. Earlier, Rajendran and the vendor engineer would supervise routine daily problems, whereas I was free to devote my time to other things. Now, under the changed scenario, almost all of my entire time was spent in solving day-to-day problems and keeping a vigil over every activity of our group.

Almost three weeks had passed since Rajendran had left, when one day the DFO called me, 'I have called you for two things. One, I have received a letter from the Lucknow Circle that you have not replied to their letter asking for your explanation in the car loan case. And two, more importantly, we have been again given notice by the union for a one-day strike on the 12th of next month, almost one month from now, against the shifting of some operations to Mumbai. The central office is planning to shift some of the operations in phases, from the 16th of next month. So get ready for the 12th and tell the others too. There will be no leaves sanctioned, at all at that point of time. Still, if somebody is absent during that period, stringent disciplinary action would be taken against him. We have to arrange and do as we did the last time during the strike.'

And after a pause added, 'And yes, what is the status and progress of our local Salt Lake contingency site? Is it ready for the operations? At what stage is it?'

'Sir, after Rajendran left, the implementation work of the site has suffered quite a bit, as I am not able to devote myself completely to it. Apart from this, the vendor engineer is also new and not even conversant with the day-to-day operations. So, most of my time is spent on those,' I apprised him with the status.

'But we have to complete it, and in any case before the strike. I am trying to get someone from the central office as a replacement for Rajendran, but then let us see. Moreover, even if everything goes well and it materializes, we won't get him so fast to assist you in this project,' the DFO clarified expressing his concern about the project.

'Sir, we will try to complete it as fast as possible, but it will expedite the process even if someone from the central office, technically conversant with it, is called temporarily on deputation basis for ten to twelve days. There are few other communication engineers of Rajendran's batch in Mumbai,' I suggested.

'Okay, I will see, but can't assure you,' the DFO said and added after a pause, 'And then you reply to the Lucknow letter.'

'For that sir, I will have to go to Lucknow to peruse some documents,' I replied.

'Then you go for a day or two. See when it is convenient for you over the next week and let me know,' the DFO said emphasising, 'But finish it now.'

'Sir, this week, and the next one some crucial hardware, including hired servers is to be installed and commissioned at the Salt Lake site and I need to be here. Let me plan it for some time over the third week from now,' I clarified.

'Okay, you let me know your final plan, but do it fast,' the DFO said finally.

'What happened to your car loan case? Have you made the paid trip to Kanpur yet?' asked Bajpai, while having tea with me.

'No, not as yet. I did not get the chance. I'm badly tied up after Rajendran left. But now a reminder has arrived for my reply,' I said.

'Then go bugger. What are you waiting for? Enjoy paid holidays with your family,' Bajpai quipped.

'In fact, that is where the hitch is. My wife has gone to

Allahabad University for a short summer course and my son is away on a summer internship in a company at Noida. So, no one is there in Kanpur at the moment,' I explained the reason and added, 'But anyway, now I am planning to go there over the third week from now, just before the proposed strike, as the DFO wants to finish it as fast as possible, and by then, at least my wife will be back in Kanpur.'

31

Before the Storm

Meanwhile, a communication engineer joined the Computers Group from Mumbai on deputation to expedite the preparation for the Salt Lake contingency site, before the proposed strike on the 12th. The programme for shifting the operations to Mumbai in phases from the 16th, had also come officially from the central office. I was totally engrossed in the implementation of the project, as only ten days were left for the D-day, when the DFO called me in the afternoon. 'See, you have not visited Lucknow yet to peruse the documents and not replied to their letter, and here I have received this nasty reminder asking you to submit your reply latest by the 10th positively. Today is 2nd so you proceed tomorrow night to Lucknow, peruse the documents on the 4th and come back on the 5th morning as your presence here is a must.'

'Sir, it will require at least two days to peruse the documents. And at this crucial juncture of commissioning, it would be difficult to be away for two days, without affecting the implementation of the project. Moreover, the communication engineer from Mumbai is here only up to the 8th and I want to finish the project before he leaves. So, if I go for two days now, it will definitely delay the project badly. I suggest sir, let me proceed on 8th evening when he too will leave and peruse the documents on the 9th and the 10th, and return on 11th morning,' I suggested.

'But will it not be too risky to go just before the proposed strike? If you are not able to return in time...for one reason or other?' the DFO expressed his concern.

'In fact, that is why I am keeping two days in Lucknow, if in case I am held up there for some reason or other. But, if I go now at such a critical juncture of the project, it will definitely have a cumulative effect on its implementation—for each day of my absence from here, it will be delayed by more than a day. So, it will not be possible to complete it by the 11th, before the strike,' I expressed my dilemma.

'Okay, then it's a compulsion and we don't have many choices. We have to complete the project before the 11th and you have to reply to their letter also latest by 10th or at least mark your presence there to peruse the documents. So, it is a deadlock. Then you plan as you suggest, but make sure you are here on 11th morning in any case,' said the DFO after a while, weighing various pros and cons.

'And one more thing,' added the DFO in a cautioning low tone, 'Be careful, these people can go to any extent. I have heard that they can sabotage the contingency site...or even physically harm some of us...So personal security first...'

In the evening, at my home, I received a phone call from Mr Kaushik Mukherjee, my neighbour's relative from Kanpur.

After exchanging usual greetings, he said, 'See, I had told you that they would try to reopen the case with the police. Luckily, sir, it fizzled out. But they are very dangerous people, and can go to any extent with their evil designs. First, they took that girl's life through that vendor engineer, and when the engineer threatened to get out from their captivity and disclose all this to the world, he was also killed.'

He further cautioned me, 'I have heard that they are planning to physically obstruct people from entering the office on the strike day, or even from the night before so that the people, critical to the operations, should not reach in advance, as it happened last time. Be careful sir, they may even try to physically harm...The best thing for you is to take leave and proceed to Kanpur.'

'But nobody will be granted leave for that period and if somebody still remains absent, then stringent action would be taken against him,' I said.

'But you can always proceed to Kanpur for some urgent personal reasons after intimating them, whether they sanction leave or not. It has to be sanctioned later,' he advised.

'Thank you so much Mr Mukherjee for the concern and cautioning me. I will definitely keep these things in my mind,' and I disconnected the call.

32

The D-Day

As planned, I proceeded to Lucknow on 8th night, reached on 9th morning for the perusal of car loan documents. Surprisingly, on my way, I received an anonymous call warning me not to return before the 12th in my own interest. I remained quite busy throughout the day in my work, except for the few interruptions when I received calls from the FTMO Cal for something or other related to the project or concerning the preparations for the ensuing strike. As such, there was nothing in the case to peruse, but still to complete the exercise and more importantly, to mark my presence at the Vigilance Department, CHO Lucknow before the 10th, assuaging their ego, I had to go. In the evening, I was sitting with my friends, when I received a daily routine call from my wife. She had just reached Kanpur from her short summer course at Allahabad. I told her that I would be reaching Kanpur the next day on the 10th in the evening to catch the Rajdhani Express for Cal in the night. In passing, she told me that our son, who was undergoing summer internship at Noida, had been a little low that day, when she spoke to him.

The next day, I finished my job fast, as there was nothing much to check, and proceeded to Kanpur in the afternoon. I was nearing Kanpur, when I received a call from my wife saying that she had just received a call from my son's company, informing that he was seriously ill, suffering from severe dehydration and was being shifted, to a Delhi hospital. I told her that I was about to reach Kanpur and we would immediately catch the Shatabdi Express at 4.40 p.m., for Delhi. It was the earliest possible connection for Delhi. A flight from Lucknow would have taken the same time or more.

I immediately called the DFO secretariat and told them about the position, asking them to connect me to the DFO. When the DFO came on the line and I told him about this development, the phone went completely silent. There was no response from the other side. I then immediately called his personal secretary and explained the situation. I further advised him to discuss with the DFO to immediately call the communication engineer the next day from Mumbai, who had been there with us until the 8th and was conversant with the operations of our Salt Lake contingency site.

We reached the hospital at night. He was in the ICU and his condition was still serious, though stable. The next day on the 11th also, though he was responding to the treatment, his condition was still not good enough to be discharged from the ICU. So, it seemed to be out of question to catch either a train or a flight for Cal and be there on the 12th.

I called the DFO's PS in the afternoon and told him that my last hope of reaching there on the 12th morning was almost over and now as things stood, it would be impossible for me to be there on the D-day. I asked the status of the Mumbai communication engineer and was told that immediately after reporting at the central office on the 9th, he had proceeded on leave to his home in Ahmedabad. Though the DFO had reservations in calling him from home, but anyway he had been summoned and hopefully, should be there on the 12th, the PS further added.

Meanwhile, fortunately, my son's condition improved dramatically and late in the evening, he was discharged from the ICU to a regular ward. When I asked him, he said that he was all right, and I could leave. Doctors also said that now there was no problem and he was recovering very fast, when I consulted them. I decided to leave for Cal by the early morning flight the next day, which was to reach there around 8'o clock.

The next day, on the 12th, total anarchy broke out at the FTMO, as the striking staff from very early morning, obstructed people from entering the office by manhandling them. Some of them were even taken as hostages. There was utter chaos and total disruption of the operations. In the melee, some people were injured, and were hospitalized. Some of their leaders were taken into police custody for inciting the violence. But they succeeded in stopping the functioning for the time being. I landed at Cal unannounced around 8:30 a.m. Knowing the position at the FTMO, over the mobile, I directly proceeded to the Salt Lake contingency site. After some time, the communication engineer from Mumbai also joined me and by 10' o clock we could start all the essential operations from there. We heaved a long sigh of relief, as we managed to maintain our presence in the global markets and thus save our reputation and pride. Few more people, who could not enter the FTMO, also joined us later, at Salt Lake. Of course, full-fledged operations of the FTMO were disrupted, but we could still maintain essential operations, from Salt Lake. It was a matter of great satisfaction that I had reached there and could join my duties in times of need. Moreover, the site could be run successfully. The striking people, of course, once again could not succeed in their motives. My not being there on the previous evening, perhaps, proved a boon in disguise for us, as the people were misled and had focused all their attention at the FTMO. Moreover, I could directly go to the site without being harmed or held up. In the evening, I called the DFO from the Salt Lake site to take his permission to leave for Delhi, at night and he happily agreed. Of course, all through the day he was in touch with us over the phone and wanted to know what time we had started receiving transaction strings from the branches.

I reached Delhi quite late in the night, so to say, early hours of the 13th morning. My son was finally discharged from the hospital on the14th. I decided to directly take the Rajdhani Express from Delhi to Cal, dropping my wife and son on the way at Kanpur. By the time, I reported at the FTMO on the 15th, things had already normalized. Only thing that had changed in between was that the staff union secretary of the FTMO was removed from his post for mishandling the issue, and also named in the FIR, lodged by the administration. He was also issued a disciplinary memo for misconduct and unruly behaviour.

In the evening, I received a phone call from Mr Kaushik Mukherjee, who like a victor very happily said, 'You did the right thing by remaining away, as I advised you. As you must know, here some people were badly manhandled and were seriously injured. Anyway, some operations, somehow, were managed from Salt Lake. Perhaps, some people came directly there from the central office Mumbai.'

In fact, he was not aware that I had come for a day in between and had directly gone to Salt Lake, from where I had managed the essential operations.

In retrospect, I felt that it was all predestined and was good that I had left for Lucknow only after completing the job of the Salt Lake site.

33

Nothing Can Be as Crafty

Before I reported at the FTMO on the 15th, Das had already left for Mumbai with the DFO the next day, immediately after the strike, as he was to coordinate and supervize the proposed shifting. I could not meet Bajpai on the 15th since both of us were completely engrossed with the shifting the next day. As planned and scheduled, the proposed shifting started from the 16th, when Mr Sikdar's body was found hanging from the ceiling of his house. It was said that he was running into heavy debts.

Meeting me after the incident Bajpai asked me, 'What do you have to say now? Was he also involved in the scam plan?'

'Yes very much. Now things are more or less clear, and all the events put together are making sense, as every bit has almost fallen in place, completing the picture. But first, you come to my department as I have to share and discuss something vital to the case,' I said tapping on his shoulder.

'Aare kuch bataoge bhi!' said Bajpai little anxiously.

'Yes-yes, why not? That is why I am taking you to my department. I want to show you a rejected string report.'

'So what is unusual about it?'

'It is not the usual rejected string report of "junk" inputs, but a computer report of a rejected forex credit transaction.'

'What?'

'Yes. Moreover, it is from Sikdar's Reconciliation Dept and strangely, it is from the day of the strike.'

'Striking day, when no department was functioning at the FTMO.'

'Yes. That is what is very unusual.'

'But you did not tell me earlier.'

'This happened on the 12th when I left for Delhi in the evening directly from the Salt Lake contingency site and after that I returned only yesterday on 15th when both of us were busy with the shifting. Where was the chance to share this information with you?'

'True.'

'Since it could not be matched, it is in a raw string form. But it seems there is only one transaction in the string. Since you have worked in that department, perhaps, you can throw some light. Moreover, in your present cover department, you have access to account numbers of all Indian as well as foreign clients, dealing in forex. So it will help.'

'You mean to say you want to decipher the string?' said Bajpai amazingly.

'Yes, don't get unnerved. You just help me out.' We took a printout of the report to Bajpai's Cover Dept.

'See, it is a very short string, perhaps of only one transaction.'

'But boss, it is Greek to us. What we can make out from this long string of "zeros" and "ones"?' Bajpai frowned.

'In fact, these innocuous looking 'zeros' and 'ones' contain very vital information. We know that the first 32 bits from the right side represent the number of the account to be credited and next ones contain the amount to be credited and last 32 bits denote the creditor, and this pattern repeats in the string for different transactions. Since it is a very short string, it seems to contain information about one transaction only. We will take the first 32 bits from the right-side of the string and since it is in binary-coded decimal form, we will convert it to decimal form to find the account number and then find out the name of the account from the list of clients in your computer.'

'Are you going to convert thirty-two bits into decimal account number? And even if you are able to convert, how will it help in the case?' asked Bajpai doubting the efficacy of the entire exercise.

'See, it is not that difficult to convert. In fact, thirty-two bits represent eight unique sets or groups of four bits each. Each set of four binary bits represents one decimal digit from zero to nine, thus thirty-two bits have eight sets of four binary bits, representing an eight-digit account number. Moreover, it can be easily done through a computer. But I don't want to decipher and check it through the computer, as I unnecessarily don't want the string to figure in the "check" report and go into records. As far as the utility of this exercise is concerned, it will help us in knowing the details of the account, and confirming my worst suspicion of Sikdar's involvement in it.'

'Oh, I see. Then should we try?' muttered Bajpai.

'Yes. Let us take the first thirty-two bits from right and then split these into sets of four bits each, and covert each set into equivalent decimal digit. So the string of first thirty-two bits from the right is 00000000000000101000001001000101, which after splitting into sets of four bits each will be—0000 0000

0000 0010 1000 0010 0100 0101. These sets are converted into equivalent decimal digits of 0, 0, 0, 2, 8, 2, 4, 5 respectively as per the Conversion Table* and put together form the number of 00028245. Now from the list of foreign clients accounts in your computer, find the name of the account by putting in the account number 00028245.'

On putting in the number 00028245, the computer screen beamed:

NO ACCOUNT EXISTS FOR THE NUMBER
'There is no account for such number,' Bajpai commented gravely.
'Hmm... Query "Why?"' I asked Bajpai after a pause.

As soon as, Bajpai queried 'Why', it beamed:

EITHER NO ACCOUNT OR INVALID ACCOUNT NUMBER
I thought for a while and then at once asked Bajpai excitedly, 'Let us count the total number of bits in the string. Are they 98 instead of 96 (32 multiplied by 3) assumed by us?'
'Yes, they are 98,' we uttered in unison after counting.
'Got it,' and I mocked a punch in the air. 'In fact, the first bit of "one" on the rightmost side represents the beginning of the string and the last bit of "zero" at the leftmost side represents the end of the string. So the first and the last bits are not the part of actual transactions details and not to be taken for transactions details. So leave the first bit of "one" in the extreme right and then take 32 bits from right for the account number,' I explained.

'Good. So now after leaving the first bit of "one" on the extreme right of the string, the next 32 bits are 100 00000000000010100000100100010 or 1000 0000 0000 0001 0100 0001 0010 0010 after grouped as sets of four bits each,' Bajpai added.

'These sets get converted into equivalent decimal digits of 8, 0, 0, 1, 4, 1, 2, 2 respectively as per the Conversion Table* and put together form the decimal number of 80014122. See if some foreign client account exists for this number of 80014122.'

As soon as Bajpai put in 80014122 as account number into computer, it beamed:

BLUE STONE PRIVATE EQUITY AND INVESTMENT FIRM, NEW YORK

'Great!' we exclaimed in excitement.

'So far so good. Now let us work on the next 32 bits to find the amount of the transaction. Again, 32 bits represent eight unique sets of 4 bits each. Each set of four binary bits represents one decimal digit from 0 to 9, thus 32 bits having eight sets of 4 binary bits represent 8 digits number. But now for decoding the amount of the transaction, the first digit from right side expresses number of zeros to be suffixed (or power of 10 to be multiplied with) to the number arrived at from the remaining 7 digits,' I explained the machine coding system. 'Read out the next 32 bits after leaving first 33 bits from right. It is easier to read out from the right side and I will also write from the right side,' I told Bajpai.

'We have next 32 bits of 00000000000000000000001010 0000110 or 0000 0000 0000 0000 0000 0101 0000 0110 after splitting into sets of 4 bits each,' replied Bajpai. 'This gets converted into 8 digit number of 00000506 as per the Conversion Table*. Now taking the last digit of "6" as number of zeros, that is 00,00,00, to be suffixed to the remaining seven digit number of 0000050, we arrive at a figure of 50,00,00,00... Wow, fifty million dollars.'

'That is a huge amount... By the way, it could have been represented as the eight digits number of 5000002 which also boils down to same figure of 500000,00,' Bajpai observed.

'Yes, very true. It could have been represented in many other ways, but normally the transactions are in the scale of million dollars, so they are mostly represented in terms of millions,' I clarified.

'Great, what next?'

'Now, we should find the creditors account number, through the next 32 bits. This is to be worked out in the same way, as we did for the beneficiary account. Read out the next 32 bits leaving 65 bits from the right. Since there are only 98 bits of one transaction only, you may as well take 32 bits from the left after leaving the leftmost bit of "0".'

'00010000000000000011001010000100 or 0001 0000 0000 0000 0011 0010 1000 0100 after breaking into groups of 4 bits each,' replied Bajpai.

'This gets converted into decimal number of 10003284 as per the Conversion Table*. Find the name of the account by keying in account number 10003284 in your computer.'

When Bajpai put in 10003284 as account number into computer, it flashed:

GROW WELL FINANCES, BURDWAN, INOPERATIVE ACCOUNT

'So had we tried deciphering the string through a computer, it would have given the same details of failed transaction as:

BENEFICIARY: BLUE STONE PRIVATE EQUITY
AND INVESTMENT FIRM, NEW YORK
AMOUNT: $50 MILLION
CREDITOR: GROW WELL FINANCES, BURDWAN,
INOPERATIVE ACCOUNT,' confirmed Bajpai.
'Very correct...,' I nodded.

'Great. So this is it,' I exclaimed, 'As a last attempt, he tried to siphon off huge funds by transferring this way and pay off his debts.'

'You mean to say that he wanted to fraudulently transfer these funds and was thoroughly involved beyond doubts,' commented Bajpai.

'Yes. Firstly, the string was originated from his department and on the day of the strike when no department at the FTMO Cal was functioning. Secondly, the creditor account is some inoperative account of a firm from Burdwan, where his family originally belonged to. Then funds through fictitious entry were being transferred to a well-known investment firm of New York. In fact, he must already have an exposure through

Blue Stone Private Equity firm. If you remember, he had also visited New York, while on his LFC, perhaps to initiate his dealings with them. When he ran into huge losses in the Indian stock market, he must have thought of recouping it through fraudulently transferring funds. And for this, which could have been the better account than the account of this private equity firm, with whom he already had dealings. Being an account of a reputed investment firm, nobody would have suspected a scam in crediting this huge a sum. Moreover, such fraudulently generated funds could not have been better deployed than as further investment in this famous firm. So he planned and tried to scam by fraudulently crediting this firms account—earlier by mirroring the monitoring terminal and now this way.'

'But why fifty million dollars, which is a huge amount?' asked Bajpai.

'Because generally these big private equity firms do not accept any investment less than to the tune of fifty million dollars. Moreover, apart from recouping his huge losses in forex deals and share markets, he had to recover his other expenses also-such as in acquiring high-end software and in supporting union activities etc. Perhaps, he was betting on horse races as well. But at the same time, this amount could not be more than fifty million dollars, as he was well aware that for any amount above fifty million dollars a separate confirmation would be sent. So he played very safe.'

'But how he could generate and transmit a fictitious entry?' Bajpai was amazed at the Sikdar's ingenuity.

'It is really amazing that he had such deep and intricate knowledge of computer functioning. Though I had seen the depth of his computer knowledge earlier also, when a fire had broken out in the Cover Dept, and he could make the alternate system up in no time, but I had never imagined that he had such knowledge. In fact, the fictitious entry string must have been generated and uploaded in machine language and transmitted through the File Transfer Protocol (FTP). As you know, he had been involved with the FTMO software from the very beginning, from the selection to the purchasing stage. Not only that, he was also associated in the implementation of the software, supervizing the customization of the software, before I joined the FTMO. Therefore, he must be quite abreast with the software and deeply aware with all its nuts and bolts, intricacies, may be even know its object code. That must have helped him in fine-tuning, generating, and uploading the fictitious entry. He must have thought that on the day of the strike there would be no incoming string at the FTMO server from the branches, and this string would pass to the gateway server without validation, as there was nothing to validate with. But he did not realize that we had already booted the mirror server of the Salt Lake contingency site and had started receiving the branches strings. As the FTMO server functions were taken over by the contingency site server, this string was directed to that server and when it could not be validated there, it was rejected. Perhaps, he never thought of such a possibility and must have been sure that Blue Stone account was credited on that day. He must have realized of this fiasco later on communicating with them and then, coming to know that we had worked from the Salt Lake site. Now, sure of the revelation of his identity in the scam, on one hand, and no chance of recovery from heavy debts on the other, he was left with not many choices, finally resulting in suicide.'

'So this not only proves and confirms his involvement in the scam beyond doubt, but basically shows it was his brainchild. Hats off to Sikdar's crooked mind! But I must say you have sharper observation and analytic powers, cracking the mystery,' applauded Bajpai.

'I think, basically, we have been able to crack the mystery due to our earlier server room misadventure and experience, when we tried to watch the porno graphic sites from outside the room, by fiddling with the monitoring terminal. This experience only led us to sniffing and ultimately unfolding the scam. See, how ironic it is that the craze for the porno graphic site led us to uncover a high-level scam for defrauding, and consequently saving us from lot of untold problems. In a way, it became a boon in disguise.'

'True, but still, no doubt, you have keen observing power.'

'In fact, after the server room episode I followed each and every report generated by the computers very closely and noticed a sudden spurt in the rejected "junk" string reports of Sikdar's department. If you remember, I mentioned this rise in the "junk" reports in the last FTMO review meeting also. I was wondering about this sudden spurt, when there was no change in his department. As you know, these reports are generated mostly because of wrong inputs. This happens when either the operator is new or the job he is doing is new. But neither was applicable to his department. Now it can be easily said that all along he was trying to generate the fictitious credit entry, which could be uploaded later. And he succeeded in creating one!'

'Great! ...With this revelation, what do you have to amend and say about your earlier inferences and versions of the previous plot?' asked Bajpai.

'Now things are very clear and every bit has fallen into place completing the picture of the previous plot. Firstly, now it has been proved beyond doubts, that both the plans were his— one was his individual actual scam plan for siphoning off funds through mirroring the monitoring terminal, and the other one was a cover up for this sinister plan in association with the union people. He laid out his scam plans very intelligently and meticulously. He knew that if somehow he could control the functioning of the monitoring terminal from outside the server room, it would be very easy to transmit any fictitious entry without any checks or validation, as it was directly going to the gateway server, from the monitoring terminal. To control the monitoring terminal from outside, some suitable mirroring software was required, for which he raised queries with various vendors. In fact, he was the person, who had contacted various vendors, including the one agent in Ahmedabad, through his principal at Singapore. Then in all possibility, he bought the high-end fully functional software from Singapore, while there for reconciliation of entries, immediately after swapping position with you from head of Cover Dept to Reconciliation Dept. To control the monitoring terminal from outside, not only some mirroring software was required, but also someone competent enough was needed to install it inside the most secured server room and link it to the terminal outside. For this who could be a better choice than the vendor engineer, who had free access to do all this and was aware of every Rajendran's movement? So, he roped in the vendor engineer for this, who was well accustomed with the server room and could handle the mirroring software as well, with the same ease. But, the vendor engineer was aware of the webcam recording on the monitoring terminal, so the girl was brought in to sit on the terminal and actually operate it under the engineer's direction. To cover up and give effect to his sinister plan for this scam, he camouflaged it with the union people's plans of maligning Computers Group by breaching the most restricted area of the server room. It was timed for that day, as the vendor engineer was well aware of Rajendran's programme in advance. Now the events of the fateful day are very clear and can be easily sequenced:

- The door of the server room was left open from 3.50 to 5.55 p.m., as per the door movement log.
- The vendor engineer came out of the server room with Rajendran at 3.50 p.m., but had inserted some wedge- like thing between the door and its frame while leaving to block the door from being latched completely. When Rajendran had left and after some time I went to your department, he sneaked in with the girl in our absence. As the door was not locked, so no key was required to enter this time.
- As the engineer was aware of the recording camera, he must have put it off, before embarking on his mission of sending duplicate entries from the terminal outside. This was also evident from the recordings of the original stick, as I saw no recording of any activity prior to 5.55 p.m., while copying it on another stick, after the incident that day.

- As per the door movement log of the server room, it was open from 3.50 to 5.55 p.m., when, Rajendran had left and I was with you to wish you happy holidays. They must have installed the mirroring software, linked, sent duplicate entries, then delinked and uninstalled the software; moving to and fro from the server room to the terminal outside unhindered. If you remember, Mr Sikdar had also come there to say goodbye to you but in fact, he was there to keep a tab on me and hold me there for some more time. In fact, he had also said that he wanted to show me some reconciliation entries at his department. But, later, since I already had stayed back at your department for pretty long, he did not need to buy more time for the engineer to work in the server room.

- After finishing his job by 5.55 p.m., the engineer must have tried to switch on the camera to get the DFO's attention, but it could not be switched on unless the door was closed. Perhaps, they were not aware of this fact. Given the choice, the engineer would have made a slip at this stage, without completing the union plan, as his main plan of sending duplicate entries was over. But he could not do so since all along the union people were there to keep a tab on him. So, he had no choice but to close the door and complete the union plan. Once the door was closed and the camera was switched on, there was no way for them to get out of the server room without inserting the smart card, which they did not have. As per the plan, the DFO was to be informed about the server room happenings, right after them leaving the server room. Then, the union people would have confidently told the DFO that this was a breach of the server room by Rajendran's girlfriend and Rajendran, blaming him squarely and in turn the Computers Group directly. Anyway, the server room was accessed through Rajendran's key and that was why the DFO on reaching the room immediately asked for Rajendran, and suspected that he was there with a girl. Moreover, earlier too, once Rajendran had been found with his girlfriend in the computers' dump room and the DFO was aware of this incident. Thus, then the case would have carried a lot of weight, when the DFO would have reached the room, once the engineer and girl had left. But now in the changed situation, with the door being locked, their plan of leaving the room before the DFO arrived, misfired. They could not run away without the server room being opened from the outside. They had no option, but to wait for me to reach the department. And when I reached the department, Sikdar and the others informed the DFO about the server room activities. On opening of the server room door in the presence of the DFO, they were found embracing each other, perhaps only to misguide us again. In fact, Sikdar had also accompanied the DFO and came up to the nineteenth floor, but stayed back in the corridor outside the computers department. When the girl ran towards the staircase, he was there in the gallery and he himself bumped off the girl, as part of his original plan to misguide the people and distract any attention, from his sinister scam plan. And perhaps, as part of his momentary decision also to avoid her identification, and help the engineer to make slip out in the melee.

Swindling away the recording stick and sending it to the police was part of his plan B. When his original plan misfired, he did not lose hope. In fact, I remember that he appeared to be very happy and relaxed, when the news of the detection of the duplicate entries by our New York office broke out, as it confirmed that his scheme had worked. He still hoped that he would be able to get rid of us by implicating us, through the recording stick and would later siphon off the funds, through the monitoring terminal. But as luck would have it for him, the recording stick did not work due to Rajendran's ingenuity. When Sikdar's this plan too did not work, and no hope was left to implement his scam, through the monitoring terminal, the engineer became a burden and a great risk. So at this stage he too was eliminated. Moreover, by now he would have also come to know that there were doubts about his involvement in swindling away the recording stick. This must have made him more cautious, resulting in the annihilation of the engineer to avoid any further risk.

But he still did not lose hope of siphoning off funds, as he badly needed them. He thus came up with a very ingenious idea of doing it on the day of the strike by generating a fictitious entry, as we saw just now. But he did it as his last desperate attempt, as he knew very well about the risk involved, and the resulting consequences if it failed.'

'Mr Sikdar had a very comfortable and settled life. But due to recent developments in the office, one after the other, his life had got totally disrupted. He was under great pressure. He had a large exposure and heavy stakes in the share market, since he was also investing the money deposited with him by others for purposes, apart from managing stock portfolios for some other people. He was also investing in the forex deals, utilizing insider information and tips, gathered in his official capacity at the FTMO. He was very disturbed because of the proposed shifting of the FTMO from Cal to Mumbai, as he knew very well that without privy to such information, it was unthinkable to survive in the highly volatile forex market, and so he did not want to part away from the FTMO. At the same time, he could not imagine leaving this place for Mumbai due to his deep involvement in all this here. He was heavily losing in the share market for some time. Moreover, after exchanging positions with you from the head of the Cover Dept to the Reconciliation Dept, he was not privy to all that information and so started losing there in forex deals too. In fact, as you know, for some time now, he was trying to swap positions again with you to go back to the cover department. But it was yet to materialize. Meanwhile, when the writing on the wall became clear that the FTMO was going to be shifted, he became restless and thought of inciting a strike and trying this ingenious way of swindling of funds as a last resort. Feeling desperate, he, as a last attempt to recoup his financial position, conspired inciting this strike and tried transferring funds fraudulently during the strike, but that also failed. Already running neck deep into heavy debts without any chance of recovery, and now with the imminent possibility of all his deeds getting exposed, and his identity being revealed in the scam, finally resulted in him committing suicide.'

'This unfolds the scam mystery completely, but are you going to report about the scam?' asked Bajpai.

'No, and firmly so. Now there is no point in reporting the matter. We will unnecessarily entangle ourselves. The scam plan has already been foiled. He could not succeed in defrauding and there is no threat now as he is already dead. Now we will have to report the matter from the very beginning, from our observations about the first attempt for defrauding through duplicate entries, and his involvement. And as I already told you earlier, after the first attempted scam, I could not share so much with anyone, and claim that this too was possible, as no one else knew about our earlier misadventures in the server room. More so, there would have been very serious repercussions for grave dereliction of our duties in maintaining the server room's security and sanctity, if I had disclosed and elaborated this conspiracy, being solely responsible for the server room. Moreover, if now I start sharing my initial observations about the first attempt of the scam, then I will be asked why I did not share the matter earlier when I had sniffed and unfolded the plot. So the best thing is now to forget about it, otherwise, it will entrap us in endless enquiries and investigations, unnecessarily landing us in uncalled problems and jeopardizing all our future plans. Police, anyway, will investigate the matter, as it is a suicide case.'

'Yes... So the chapter is closed. Except was there somebody else also with him in the plan or at least did he have any ones silent support, who might have had heavy stakes like him?' commented Bajpai.

'I feel he could not have been alone. Surely, somebody else must also have been with him, directly or indirectly, or

at least behind him. But perhaps, that will remain a mystery,'
I quipped.

*Conversion Table

Bit	Decimal digit
0000	0
0001	1
0010	2
0011	3
0100	4
0101	5
0110	6
0111	7
1000	8
1001	9

34

And the VRS

'I have heard that you were enquiring about the modalities for voluntary retirement from admin. Are you contemplating on those lines?' asked Bajpai, while having tea at the Tea Club, a few days later.

'Yes. In fact, I had been contemplating for a long time, but was waiting for the opportune time. Now I feel I am approaching that moment,' I said.

'What do you mean by "opportune time" boss?' Bajpai asked innocently.

'By "opportune time" I mean when everything is justified at the right time, as priorities in a person's life keep on changing from time to time. So it is "opportune time" for something, when it is done at the appropriate time like having fun with playmates during childhood, being in love during youth and then building your career and family during mid-age, and still later in life, may be realize some lifetime's dream,' I explained.

'But how is it opportune time for quitting in your case?' Bajpai probed.

'See, I wanted to do something of my own, but was waiting for the right time to realize this lifetime dream of mine, when I would be relatively free from my other obligations. One may have a lifetime dream, but he can defer it for an even better time, when one becomes relatively free from other obligations of life. I have reached that "opportune time". In fact, for quite some time now, I have been feeling like quitting, but then I also wanted to complete the contingency site which was project, new and quite challenging to me. Since it has been successfully implemented, I feel I am now free of all my official obligations also. More so, we have been able to foil the scam plan as a bonus in the process. Besides, now the process of shifting the FTMO to Mumbai has also started, and as you know, Mumbai is not my cup of tea anyway,' I revealed my cards.

It had of course been my long cherished and dormant desire to do some serious writing, expressing to my feelings, reflections of life, for which I always had a strong passion, but no occasion. Earlier, though, I had written articles and short stories, which were well received and published also, I never had the chance to try my hand at writing something full length. As I had already made some progress on my book, I wanted to complete and publish it. So, it was my first task after leaving the bank. Then I also wanted to do something in my core field of engineering and technology, my first love. And with so much exposure in computers and finance, I was dying to use all my skills. As my son was about to complete his engineering degree and my wife was fully settled and engrossed in her passion of teaching, her first love, I thought it was opportune time for me to leave the bank. Moreover, my service, anyway, had become eligible for pension. Meanwhile, the car loan case against me was also dropped, as the complete outstanding was liquidated. So, I decided to submit my papers for voluntary retirement. Though earlier, I held some grudges, but with maturity and over a period of time, it mellowed down. I realized that these things happened with everyone, sometime or other during the course of the career, and were part of the game. One had to move on. I had the satisfaction that I had served the institution with best of my capabilities and came out unscathed. I was happy, as I was leaving the organisation on a positive note with lot of experiences and memories, some so sweet and some not all that sweet. But, undoubtedly, I owed a lot to the great organisation and its people!

Later searching Sikdar's house, the police recovered a note having mention of some duplicate entries and then a credit entry of fifty million dollars favouring Blue Stone Equity Firm, New York; thus corroborating with my observations and inferences, bringing the curtains down on the scam.

Epilogue

Few Weeks Later

Bajpai has come to see off Rajesh, who is finally leaving Cal after taking voluntary retirement. The train has started pulling out of the platform. Rajesh, standing pensively by the door of the train coach, waves his hand uttering, 'Only thing is who else was there with Sikdar in the scam?'

Bajpai, taking giant steps to keep pace with the accelerating train, yells out, 'Oh, you know the police have now recovered a diary from Sikdar's house with details of his deals, and the maximum deals and instructions he had from someone is a code named 8055.'

'What? Read those numerals as the closest looking alphabets to them,' Rajesh is heard saying, with bright eyes in a receding tone, as the train picks up speed.

Glossary

AMC—Annual Maintenance Contract

ATM—Automated Teller Machine

Computer network—Network of inter-connected computers and peripherals

CVC—Central Vigilance Commission, Govt of India

Circle—An independent operational unit, generally, comprising a state

CHO—Circle Head Office

Contingency site—mirror site or standby alternate site replicating the primary site with similar systems for same operations and to be used in case of emergency

DFO—Director (Foreign Operations), a very senior official, of the rank next to the Executive Director

ED—Executive Director

ES—Executive Secretary

Ethernet—Computer network using metallic coaxial cables as connecting media

LFC—Leave Fare Concession

Optic-fibre cables—Fibreglass cables using light as media of transmission, which is very fast

FBI—First Bank of India

FIR—First Information Report

FTMO—Foreign Transactions Monitoring Office of the FBI

Forex—Foreign (Currency) Exchange

IT—Information Technology
PC—Personal Computer
PO—Probationary Officer
Server—Main computer in the network
Two Bids Tender Process—Generally, a tender consists of two bids—a technical bid, providing technical specifications offered by a vendor; and a commercial (price) bid, quoting price offered by the vendor. These two bids are submitted in separate sealed envelopes by a vendor. First, the technical bids of all the vendors are opened, and then of those vendors, who qualify in their technical bids, satisfying all the tender specifications and conditions, price bids are opened.
UGC—University Grants Commission
Fatrugiri—roaming around aimlessly
Kasba—a small township
Tehmad—loincloth (wrapped around hips in folds) with both the ends stitched together
VSAT—Very Small Aperture Terminal
ZM—Zonal Manager

Author's Note

Postscript:

Some issues to ponder on-

1. Whether people associated with the implementation of the system to continue with its operations also later.

    Upside—easy to run the show for the persons abreast with the system

    Flip side—easier to fiddle around the system for the persons knowing its nut-bolts

2. To what extent maintenance of the system is handed to external agencies

3. System to be audited thoroughly and regularly from time to time by third party so that its absolutely secured and tamper-proof at all levels.

A word of disclaimer–

This is a work of fiction and has nothing to do with any actual financial system, being purely the product of the author's imagination. Names, characters, places, and incidents too either are the product of the author's imagination or are used fictitiously, and any resemblance to any actual persons, living or dead, events or locales, is entirely coincidental.

Acknowledgements

To say the least, this project would not have taken shape without support and encouragement from various quarters, especially my friends and family members who have stood by all my idiosyncrasies with a smile. I'd like to thank numerous persons associated, directly or indirectly, with the book and in particular:

- Readers of my first book who have inspired me to write this book, especially Messrs Pattabhi Raman, Anil Bansal, Anag Desai, Kajal Ghose, Gautam Mukherjee, Mauli Shankar Rao, Suplab Das, Rajeev Tewari (Dr), Ramesh Mehta (Col), Ravi Jain; Pratiti Hazarika, Rukmini Vedula, Hema B, Anjli Prakash to name a few, for their valuable feedbacks.
- My family and friends for their constant support and cheering me up all the time, particularly my wife Sindhu, son Abhinav and daughter-in-law Tanu and the entire family—*Mausi* Savitri Jain; siblings Dr Subhash–Sudha, Usha, Dr Aditya–Nita, Neeraj–Richa, Rajiv–Sunita, Neeraj–Anita, Pankaj–Mamta, Neelu–Ravi; The gen-next—Akshay–Sikha, Atul–Jyoti, Amit–Alka, Avni–Mukul, Atashi–Priyendra, Sumeet–Priya, Suchi–Arif, Natalie, Priyanka, Udit, Aproov, Mayank, Mohit, Nischaya, Neha, Swati, Shweta, Pulkit and the

  dear young ones—Vanessa, Sherry, Harsh, Khushi, Atij, Ishaan, Armaan, Kovil, Zakir, Nitin and Radha.

- My publishers and their entire team at Rupa Publications for all their support without which there would have been no book.
- It is not possible to acknowledge everyone individually, nonetheless I am highly indebted to all who have contributed and inspired me at some point of time or other in some way or another.

Finally, I am fortunate to have the blessings of all my elders, particularly my father late Shri C.L. Jain, mother late Smt. Rishi Devi Jain, uncle late Shri Manik Chandra Jain, eldest brother late (Brig.) Anand Mohan Jain, father-in-law late (Col) Mahesh Chandra Jain and mother-in-law late Smt. Sarojini Devi Jain. Everything that is mine is because of the All Pervasive, All Kind, Shirdi Sai Baba.